BORN IN THE APOCALYPSE

JOSEPH TALLUTO

D1306417

SEVERED PRESS
HOBART TASMANIA

BORN IN THE APOCALYPSE

Copyright © 2016 Joseph Talluto
Copyright © 2016 Severed Press

WWW.SEVEREDPRESS.COM

All rights reserved. No part of this book may be
reproduced or transmitted in any form or by any
electronic or mechanical means, including
photocopying, recording or by any information and
retrieval system, without the written permission of
the publisher and author, except where permitted by law.

This novel is a work of fiction. Names,
characters, places and incidents are the product of
the author's imagination, or are used fictitiously.
Any resemblance to actual events, locales or persons,
living or dead, is purely coincidental.

ISBN: 978-1-925493-10-8

All rights reserved.

CHAPTER 1

"Do you think it's one of them?"

"I dunno. Has it moved?"

"Not for the last ten minutes."

"How do you think it got here?"

"Dunno. Was it here before?"

"Don't remember seeing it, but the wind last night might have blown the leaves off it."

"Throw something at it."

"*You* do it."

My friend Trey Chambers and I were looking at a body. It was a middle-aged man about forty five, although my only reference to middle-aged men was Mr. Greyson over the ridge. It looked about as old as him and about the same color, so maybe it was all right. It was lying on its side under a holly bush with its arms crossed on its chest and its head was turned away from us.

"Should we go around it, look at it from the front?" Trey asked.

"Well, we have to if we want to get home," I said. We'd been hunting for the better part of the morning, checking our snares and having a fair amount of luck. We had three rabbits apiece, and I had an extra squirrel I managed to knock out of a tree with a well-thrown rock. We had seen the tracks of a deer, but we had nothing on us that would take down a large animal. We had our packs and our knives, but that was it.

We walked carefully through the brush, trying to keep to the game trail that ran a zig-zag pattern through the woods. Behind our houses was a decent-sized forest, and we had both grown up exploring and hunting its depths. There wasn't much to the forest we hadn't seen, so to come across this body suddenly was having to admit it wasn't there before. And in that case, there was a really good chance it was one of *them.*

We slowly walked around the man, trying to see its face before it saw us. If it was one of them, it would have dark splotches all over its face. If it wasn't, it would look normal. That was the easiest way to tell, although not all of them had the splotches. A few were normal-looking, and you couldn't tell they were a problem until they tried to get you.

Trey bumped my arm. I looked over at him, and he pointed to the body once, then pointed to his own eyes. He shook his head, and I took him at his word. I couldn't see the face at the angle I was at, being taller than he was, but Trey was telling me he didn't think it was one. We'd seen them before, and we knew what they could do, so we were naturally cautious about approaching one. We'd also seen plenty of dead bodies as well, so if this was another one of *those*, no big deal.

We worked our way across the path and moved away from the body. I'd tell my dad about it, and he would probably come out and drag it over to the burn hole. It was a deep pit about fifty feet across and was originally thirty feet deep. It had started out as a retention pit for the floods we would get, but it served another purpose in the end.

"Hey, Josh?" Trey said as we followed the trail again.

Whatever I was thinking of answering flew out of my head as the bush over the body suddenly exploded in sound and flying leaves. The corpse, which it now obviously it wasn't, thrashed and tore at the clinging shrub as it tried to free itself.

Trey and I took one look at the monster coming after us, and we didn't have to think twice. We turned and ran for our lives.

Behind us, the infected person tore free of the foliage and came after us in the typical fast walk of someone who had fallen prey to the disease that had killed so many. It seemed they couldn't quite work out the mechanics of running, but walking fast was the next best thing. Of course, when you were twelve years old like Trey and I were, a fast walking adult was almost on par with as fast as we could run.

"Go, go, go!" I yelled, pushing Trey on. He was the slower of the two of us and the most likely to trip on something. If he had been behind me he wouldn't have made it. I could hear the man stumbling, wheezing, and trying like crazy to get at us. If we fell or stopped, he'd tear us apart.

"Where can we go?" Trey yelled, running past a small stand of trees. That was a landmark for us and told us we were close to our homes.

"Head down the hill; we'll get him with the rocks!" I panted, stealing a look behind me and wishing immediately I hadn't. The man was moving fast, and his walk was pretty steady, which on these people meant he had been infected fairly recently, and his mind still remembered how to move. Thank God he had forgotten how to run.

"Are you nuts?" Trey wheezed, turning left anyway. "We'll get in trouble for sure!"

"Gotta risk it unless you want to run forever," I said, moving down the hill. The forest we emerged from led out onto a huge man-made hill which extended for a quarter mile in front of us. The top was flat and grassy, and the sides were steep enough to give even a healthy person a case of the heaves. Going up was hard enough, but going down was a piece of cake. We just let gravity take over and slid down the grass until we reached the rocks at the bottom.

The rocks themselves were huge, the smallest of them being larger than my fist. The larger ones we couldn't even move if we tried together. But we didn't need those, we just needed ones that were about the size of a pumpkin. Trey and I each picked up a rock the size of a shoebox and lay in wait for the diseased man to come tumbling down.

We heard him before we saw him. Those infected with the Tripp Virus wheezed a lot since we were told they were missing a lot of their lung tissue, and their throats were messed up. It wasn't too bad in the daylight, but at night it really creeped me out.

In a minute, the man walked off the edge of the hill, and fell right onto his face. He slid that way for a while and wound up crashing head first into the same rock pile we did. Blood poured out of a deep gash on his cheek, and the impact stunned him just enough for us to move.

"Get him!" I yelled at Trey, heaving my rock up and dumping it on the prone man's shoulders. The man wheezed suddenly and tried to turn his head, but it was wedged in between two rocks and not going anywhere.

Trey tossed his rock onto the man's back, and then jumped on top of the rocks, adding his weight to the stones. The combined heaviness was too much for the infected man, and he couldn't do anything but lay there and bleed.

Trey looked over at me. "You gotta kill him, man!"

I looked down at the pathetic creature with a mixture of loathing, disgust, and fear. I had seen these things since the day I was born, and I never got used to them. But that didn't stop me from doing what needed to be done, and I picked up the biggest rock I could lift. Pushing it over my head, I brought it down with both hands onto the head of the infected man. The rock cracked into the man's skull, stunning him, and I lifted the rock and brought it down again. This time there was a serious crack as the rock broke the skull and penetrated the brain. The man's thrashing ceased, and lay there as blood leaked out of his head and stained the rocks around him.

Trey climbed off, and we looked down at the dead man.

"That was close, man," Trey said.

I nodded. "Yeah, but we got this," I said with bravado I didn't really feel.

"Let's get home," Trey said, looking around.

"Better get our rabbits back," I said, starting to climb up the hill. We had pitched our catch when the Tripp victim started chasing us.

"Ugh," Trey said. "I hate backtracking. Stupid Tripper."

CHAPTER 2

We called them Trippers after the virus came. According to my dad, it was a little thing that suddenly became a big problem. It started with the street junkies, the homeless, and the runaways. No one really paid any attention to the spread because it was out of sight. The way things worked, if it wasn't seen it wasn't a problem. But according to the rumors, the virus came in with a load of marijuana. It was ingested, and from there it took off in its new host. It attacked the neural pathways in the brain, causing the victim to forget everything about themselves, turning them into mindless husks. After that, it went to work on the nervous system itself, eating away at the pain receptors. People with the virus could lose a limb and not feel a thing. Finally, the virus slowed down the body systems, with the heart beating only ten or twelve times a minute. But they could still move nearly as quickly as they could before they caught the disease. The weird thing was they seemed to just keep going even after they should have died from starvation, exposure, or dehydration.

We heard the virus transferred from host to host through bodily fluids, and could live for seventy-two hours in open air. That was how it spread. The virus turned the victims into mindless, rabid animals, attacking anything they saw as a threat. My dad explained, as we learned later, that they were territorial which was why they attacked everyone they saw on their turf. Trippers, being mindless, didn't stay in one place but wandered about, which made their territory just about everywhere. They didn't attack each other, and my dad said it was because they didn't see other infected as threats. They lived in a constant state of high alert, ready to fly at anything. But all of this was just rumor; we really didn't know anything.

I didn't see any of this, because on the day I was born I saved my dad's life. My father was a policeman, and just as my mom went into labor, his station was called up to help put down an outbreak of Trippers. Every single officer who answered the call that day died. My dad called me his luck, and I suppose for that one day I was.

Dad took Mom and me home the next day, and three days later the hospital we had been in was overrun. There were too many Trippers out there to deal with, and the police couldn't handle them all. Eventually things just fell apart, and we'd been on our own ever since.

We managed better than most at first, and it was probably my dad that returned the favor by saving us all during the really bad times. Once the Trippers took over and the police were gone, people started banding together for survival. Problem was, desperate people put in desperate situations with death right around the corner tended to tear themselves apart from within. My dad told me stories about finding several groups of people all lying dead in a bunch, and it looked like they had just simply killed each other.

We probably also survived because we lived pretty far away from main population centers. We had a house on the far end of a small town with a forest in the backyard and a creek nearby. It was all I had ever known.

Trey lived across the street, and the creek that wound its way around the area went directly through his back yard. Water was never a problem for his family. Trey's mom used to be an accountant, and for lack of anything else to do, she took it upon herself to educate Trey and myself in math. Since she didn't have to follow any curriculum, we probably got a better education than we could have in the normal world. Trey's dad was a pipefitter, and before the end of civilization he had owned a small but successful business. These days, he occupied himself with figuring out how to bring more water to larger areas of growing vegetables and fruits.

I threw a wave to Trey as he headed off around the front of my house and took off for his own. I hung the rabbits from a small branch, taking care they didn't reach low enough for a scavenger to get them. I felt like I earned the jumpers today.

"Mom! I'm home!" I yelled as I entered into the garage through the side door. I took off my gear, putting everything in its proper place. Dad taught me that trick. If I ever had to leave in a hurry, and if it was dark or light, I always knew where my stuff was and could get it without delay. Dad taught me a lot of tricks. Some Mom knew about; some she was better off not knowing.

"How was the snare line?" Mom asked like she always did. I never knew if Mom actually cared about it or was just being polite. She didn't go outside much, and usually went to bed right after dark. Dad said she took the end of the world pretty hard, but I couldn't see the big deal.

"It was good; I got three decent rabbits," I said, washing my hands in the sink.

"Good for you," Mom said absently. "Are you going to clean them or let your father do it again?"

I ducked a little. "I'll go do it right now," I said, moving to the door.

"Josh?" Mom called out as I stepped into the garage.

"Yeah?"

"We can spare one of the rabbits for the Simpsons. I heard Lucy's mom isn't feeling well, and they haven't had much luck with their traps," Mom said.

"All right," I said, closing the door. Under my breath I added, "That's because they can't bait worth a damn, and their traps are too big anyway. This ain't Africa."

I spent the next hour cleaning and washing the rabbits. I didn't bring up the Tripper to my mom since she would have freaked out, and I don't need that today. I was a little shaky the more I thought about it, since I had never actually killed a Tripper before. I had seen my dad do it a hundred times, and there was that big attack where I loaded guns for my dad while the Trippers attacked the house, but I hadn't ever had to do it myself.

I didn't know what to feel about it. On the one hand, I felt glad I was alive. On the other hand, I had killed someone. I guess it would be different if I had to kill someone I knew, but I don't know. I guess it was just him or me, and I made it him.

I finished with the rabbits just in time to see my dad come back from his rounds. When everything went south, as he called it, he knew people would fall apart unless there was some kind of order being kept. So my dad, being a police officer, decided to keep his badge on and handle the normal, everyday problems that came up from people trying to survive. He didn't call himself a police officer anymore; he just called himself the Law. He wore his badge and gun, and went around the homesteads checking on people, making sure things were okay, dealing with Trippers if they showed up, and generally keeping the peace. He told me at first he was a little freaked by the responsibility, since he was essentially judge, jury, and executioner, but people seemed to realize it was necessary and were glad someone was willing to step up and do it.

I walked into the house the same time my dad did after he put up and took care of his ride.

"Hey, pal! How's things?" my dad asked me as he gave my mother a kiss. Mom's worried faced looked calmer now, like the stress of being alone was gone now that Dad was home.

"I caught three rabbits today; they're in the tank right now. Mom wants me to take one over to the Simpsons later," I said, looking up at my dad. He was a big man, broad shouldered and strong. I must have sounded different because my dad looked at me sideways and squinted slightly.

"Good for you! Let's go take a look at them and see which one we want to send to the Simpson's." My dad took me by the shoulder and led me into the garage where we kept the water tank for the cleaned kills.

We closed the door behind us and walked over to the tank. It was a small stock tank my dad picked up from somewhere, and we used it for cleaning game and keeping the flies off our kills.

I pulled out the jumpers, and dad's mouth turned down as he nodded and looked appraisingly at the rabbits. I had the pelts hanging up, and I would cure them later.

"We can give them that middle one there; that should keep them for a day," Dad said. As I put the rabbits back, Dad asked the question I worried about since this morning.

"Anything you need to tell me?" Dad asked, putting a hand on my shoulder. I was tall for my age and developing broad shoulders myself, but at the moment I felt like a three-year-old who just got caught stealing the cookies.

I looked down. "Trey and I killed a Tripper today."

CHAPTER 3

My dad took me by both shoulders and looked me in the eyes. He was as serious as I had ever seen him.

"Take me there now," he said quietly. He went over to the small locker we had by the door and pulled out a rifle. It was a simple .22 rifle, but it was all we needed for this right now. Dad had trained me on it and I knew how to use it, but I wasn't supposed to take it out unless there was an emergency. Trippers were attracted to loud noises, and gunshots seemed to make them angry. Or angrier. That was a lesson that wasn't learned early enough. Dad said all the gunshots from people and cops trying to defend themselves just made the situation worse. Crazed Trippers were not a nice thing to see.

Dad poked his head into the house to tell mom we were going to check on something, and we would be back in a few minutes. Just to keep her from worrying, Dad told me to string my bow and take it with me. I slipped the string on quickly, and threw my quiver onto my back. I loved my bow, and according to my dad I was pretty good with it. I made my own arrows and practiced whenever I could. I didn't take it with me too often to hunt because it tended to get in the way. The only time I took it hunting was when I was looking for big game like deer.

We walked across the side yard and up the steps that took us to the top of our fence. It was a tall wooden fence that Dad had reinforced with rocks over the years. It could keep out a horde of crazed Trippers and twice it had.

"Where did it come from?" Dad asked as we jumped down off the fence. We could have used the gate, but for some reason, Dad liked the steps.

"Don't know," I said, adjusting my quiver which had shifted in the jump. "Trey and I saw a body lying under a bush, and we looked close trying to see if it was a Tripper or if it was just someone who was sleeping. It chased us out of the woods."

"Did you have your bow with you?" Dad asked.

"No, just my knife. The guy was pretty big," I said.

"All right. What then?"

"Well, Trey and I slid down the north side and waited by the big rocks near the creek. The guy fell down the steep hill, but we jumped him when fell, "I said.

"What do you mean?" Dad asked sternly. "You didn't touch him yourself, did you?"

"No, Dad. Sheesh. We threw big rocks on him to keep him down, and then I crushed his skull with another rock. Trey stood on him, too. He couldn't move." I was kind of defensive about the situation, since I thought I had done pretty good.

My father thought about that one for a bit. He didn't say anything for a while, then he burst out laughing.

"That's great!" He clapped me on the back as he beamed with pride. "That took guts and brains, and I couldn't have done better myself!" He laughed again.

I felt a lot better, and actually looked forward to seeing my handiwork again.

We slipped down the small ditch, and crossed the narrow two-lane road that ran behind our house. It had been a long time since a car was on that road, and it was broken up and cracked all over. Dad said that there were roads all over the place, and you once could go anywhere in the country just by getting in your car. Our car was up on blocks with the tires off. Dad said it wasn't going anywhere anyway, and he'd probably just push it out to make room for another horse stall.

Crossing the street, Dad stopped and turned his head into the wind. He closed his eyes and listened, and I knew enough to keep quiet when he did this. He told me he was using his radar, and I figured it had to be true since we never got into trouble when he did this.

Crossing the road, we slipped through the brush and worked our way over to the rocks. There wasn't a lot of animal activity right now, and I was slightly curious as to why. We had been here so many times it was funny how the locals had adapted to us.

Getting to the rocky areas was pretty easy once we worked our way through the brush. The path I used on a regular basis was easy for me, but dad had a time because he had to get down to my height to clear the branches and brambles.

"Where is he?" Dad asked, looking around. "Never mind, I see him." Dad went over to where the body still lay, looking over the kill area, and looking up towards the top of the hill. He stepped halfway up the slope and looked down at the body from a higher angle.

For my part, I couldn't figure out what the heck he was doing. The body was right down here, right in front of me. It sure wasn't going anywhere, and it sure wasn't going to tell us where it came from. I had nothing to do but warm myself in the sun and watch the lazy water of the creek flow under the bridge and trickle out of sight around a bend. The sun bounced off the water, sending crazy reflections into the walls of the bridge.

After a minute I got bored, so I used the time to practice drawing an arrow from my quiver and nocking it. I tried to do it faster and faster, and finally quit when I lost my grip on the arrow and threw it ten yards away.

"Damn," I said as I made my way over to where I thought the arrow had gone.

"What did you say?" Dad called. He was down by the body, looking at the rocks and pulling the man over to see his face. From my angle, he didn't get better looking in direct sunlight.

"Nothing, "I said quickly. Dad didn't swear, so I ended up learning the fundamentals from Trey. Dad always said we are judged by our words and deeds, so if you may have blown it on one, you could always try to build up the other. I figured I could curse as long as I did something heroic once in a while.

I reached the spot where I thought I saw my arrow land and looked carefully for the fletching. I didn't see it right away and knelt down for another look. I swept my hand through the grass and thought I felt the shaft, but was disappointed when it turned out to be a weed.

Another sweep gave me a possibility, and I felt the stick up to the end where it flared outward in plastic fletching. I was just about to stand up and shout out my find when I saw it.

Up the road, just across the bridge, was a Tripper. It was an older one with deep red splotches on his face. His clothes were tattered like he had been outside for a long time. One foot dragged along the other, but that was a fooler. When the rage hit, they moved fast no matter how bad they were injured. There were some deep looking claw marks on his face, and dried blood crusted his neck and shoulder.

I didn't want to shout, but I had to warn my dad somehow. I looked back, and instead of seeing my father, I saw nothing at all. He was nowhere to be seen.

I didn't know what to do. I had my bow, but I'd never shot at a Tripper before. If I missed, he would be on me in seconds. I needed to be able to shoot again quickly, but I didn't know how. I was shaking as I watched the Tripper move closer and closer.

As I sat there in the brush, I realized I was concealed, and the Tripper would walk on by. Maybe I could get him from behind which would buy me some seconds if I missed if I didn't get a kill shot on the first try. I didn't have any options, I just hoped my dad wouldn't come strolling over the hill, whistling like he normally does, and get that Tripper all riled up.

It was dead silent as the infected man slowly trudged past. I could see more details, and there was a deep, black bite mark on his left arm. If I had to guess, that was where he originally got bit. It was said once you were bit, it was over for you in a matter of hours. There was no cure, and there was no vaccine. At least, we never heard of any. Dad said it was a mercy to put these poor creatures down since they were living in hell anyway. Their minds gone, their memories gone, their bodies altered and twisted. I wondered sometimes if they attacked the living in the hopes of getting killed so that they could end their suffering with a bullet to the head.

I pushed all that out of my head as I slowly made my way through the brush and grass. Years of stalking small game since the time I could walk had made me a very stealthy hunter, and I saw the Tripper as my prey now. That was the only way I could do what needed to be done without falling down in fear. Besides, my dad was probably watching, waiting for me to make a move, since his rifle would call any more Trippers to the area.

It wasn't easy crawling forward with a loaded recurve bow in my hands, but when I reached the edge of the road I was glad I had it ready since the Tripper was a lot closer than I had anticipated. I stood up on the side of the road, still partially concealed by the tall grass that grew there. Behind me was the bridge over the creek, and I could hear the water as it tumbled past the dozens of rocks Trey and I had thrown in there over the years. That sound probably had helped mask my approach, and for that I was grateful. When I realized that I could have accidentally crawled out of the grass at the feet of the Tripper, I started to sweat again.

Pulling back my arrow, I held the string for a second as I adjusted my aim. The arrow trembled slightly as the energy from the limbs prepared to launch it forward. I adjusted for the wind coming from the north and let go.

I didn't watch the arrow; I was busy whipping out another and nocking it quickly, drawing the string back, and looking for a target to come running at me. I was a bit surprised to find no target, so I eased the string forward, keeping my hand on the arrow. I stepped out of the grass and onto the road.

The Tripper lay face down in the middle of the road with his head turned to the side. Sticking out of the back of his head was my arrow. The point had gone in on the right side of the back of his skull, and the field point had blown through the bone like it wasn't there. Creeping forward, I could see the arrow tip had exited through the right eye, close to the nose. The eye was turned in my direction, almost as if it was asking me what the heck just happened.

I looked at the Tripper for a long time, not feeling anything. It was like a switch had turned off when I hunted him. It wasn't an infected person anymore, worthy of our fear and pity. It was just something I had to put down for my safety and my dad's.

Just as I was about to pull the arrow out, a voice called out of the brush.

"Leave it there."

I jumped a mile, and nearly fired an arrow at the sound, when my dad stepped out of the grass. He was holding his rifle and pointing it at the Tripper. Kneeling down, he looked over the man from head to toe, taking careful note of the two-foot pointy stick poking in and out of the man's head.

Dad looked a bit more, then scanned the area where the Tripper had come from. Seeing no danger, he stood up, and grabbing a handful of pant leg, dragged the dead man over to the side of the road.

As he worked, Dad spoke to me. "You'll have to replace that arrow, Josh. It's full of virus now, and you could get yourself infected."

I understood that thinking, as we usually washed and burned anything that had come in contact with a Tripper. I wasn't happy having to make another arrow, but I had done it before and would likely do it again. We didn't get out much to scrounge up any pre-made stuff, and when we did we were usually looking for stuff for the house. Dad was always wanting ammo and canned stuff; mom was usually looking for some sort of material. I typically grabbed whatever was shiny.

After hauling the Tripper away, Dad went and dragged the other dead man out of the rocks. He wasn't as pretty as the other guy who was sporting a new arrow through his head. This guy was bloody and flat headed from where I had pounded his skull in. Dad just grabbed another handful of leg and pulled it over the man's head, yanking him out of the rocks. Blood and brains eased out of the wound as the body was dragged through the gravel.

I was watching the proceedings with interest as I usually did with the things my Dad did. He never wasted movement, never did anything that required him to clean up later. Everything was thought out, and he always had a plan.

Once the bodies were out of the way, Dad piled a bunch of rocks on the men. It was as good a burial as they were ever going to get, since their families were probably long gone.

One thing bothered me, and I must have had a look on my face since my Dad asked me the question I had in my head.

"So why didn't I shoot him?" my dad asked me.

"Yeah!" I said, probably too loudly. "How come you let me waste an arrow?" I was focusing on the fact I had to make more arrows now.

Dad smiled. "Don't get me wrong, Josh, I would have killed him had you been in any danger. But I wanted to see if you could get close without being heard or seen, and I wanted to see if you would be able to take down a full adult with your bow."

Dad ruffled my hair a bit. "You passed on both counts. Now I know I don't have to worry about you when I'm away."

I was mollified, but still a little angry. I decided to change the subject.

"Dad?"

"What, Josh?"

"Where did he come from?" I was serious in my question. If these two Trippers were a sign of things to come, I didn't want to run into them when I ran my trap line.

Dad got a real serious look on his face. "Don't know for sure. I'm trying to figure that one out. If he came from the north, that's to be expected. But if he came from the south or west, there could be some serious trouble ahead."

"Why?"

"South means there's trouble in Manhattan and the outliers. West means there's trouble in Frankfort," Dad said simply. "The guy you took down with your bow was old, likely two to three years infected. The other guy, the first one, he probably was more fresh, and that's a worry to me."

"What can we do?" I asked, not having a clue as to where my dad was going with this.

"Well, I think the only thing to do is to track him back as far as we can, and get a general direction as to where he might have come from. After that, we check our maps and head for the towns and homes that way," Dad said.

I thought about that one. It was going to take a lot of work just for one Tripper. "Maybe he was just a roamer," I said. Roamers were just single Trippers that wandered the countryside, sometimes just laying down for a while. They were a nasty surprise when they jumped out of the grass at you. Dad nearly got killed when three of them tried to jump him. Fortunately, Dad's horse jumped away in time, and he put enough space between himself and them to get the killing shots off.

"Can't know unless we look," Dad said. "We'll start off tomorrow morning." Dad started to head across the street to the opening that led to our property.

I suddenly got excited. "I can come with?"

Dad nodded, smiling. "Of course. You're too good with your bow to leave behind. But you might want to make a few more arrows."

I walked lightly behind my Dad, my steps barely touching the ground. I had never been invited to a search before. I wondered if I should ask to bring Trey, but I decided against it. I'd rather have Trey jealous of me for a change.

Back at the house, Dad went into the stable to take care of his horse. With cars not working and electricity scarce, we made do with what was available. Dad didn't mind. He said it allowed him to slow down and make sure he didn't miss anything.

Just as I passed the door Dad turned to me. "Don't forget the rabbit for the Simpsons."

Crud. I'd hoped he had forgotten that little nugget. Oh, well. "On it. I'll be back later," I said, hauling the rabbit out of the tank and dumping it in a sack.

"Take your bow," Dad said from behind the horse. "Just in case."

I didn't know what my dad was thinking, and he didn't reveal his plans all that often, so when he did something out of the ordinary, it tended to stick out. Something was at play, and I was very curious as to what it might be. But I knew dad wasn't going to tell me, and mom sure as heck wasn't.

"Already have it," I said. I had a feeling this wasn't going to be a routine visit, and it wasn't even suppertime yet.

Crud.

CHAPTER 4

I stepped out of our property and walked along the road that connected the houses in this area. I thought it odd to have a collection of homes out in the middle of nowhere, but Dad had pointed out that when everyone had cars and gas, people drove all over the place. Living away from stores and towns was perfectly normal back then.

I wouldn't know. All I've ever known was this world where people walked or rode horses. Some people rode bicycles, and Trey's family had this bicycle car that his dad had picked up somewhere. It took two adults to make it move, so I didn't know how useful it was.

As for me, I was walking. I tied the sack to my belt so I could have my hands free, but the downside of that was the washed rabbit got my right pant leg wet from my knee down.

I passed several houses that were empty, the creepiest being the one at the bottom of a hill just three houses down from mine. Dad said when the everything went bad, that family refused to join the other families in fighting off the Trippers, and just shut themselves into their house. No one had ever seen them again. Trey said the dad went crazy and ate everyone else in there, except for his little boy, who escaped by climbing into the attic. Trey said the dad spends his time walking around the house, following the noises of the attic.

I didn't believe him, but passing by that small home tucked away in a wooded corner, I did wonder if some of the rumors were true. I'd never seen a light or movement in that house in the entire year my dad had finally let me out on my own. As I walked by, I stopped suddenly. Did a curtain move? I looked carefully from the road, but could not see any movement in any of the windows. Out of spite, I brought my bow up and drew the string back, hearing the slight rasp as the arrow slid along the shelf. I aimed at each window, daring myself to fire, but after a time I slowly eased the bow back. I shook my head, calling myself all sorts of names for my imagination.

I walked on, looking back once more. My breath caught in my throat, and I moved quickly away. In the far right window I swear I saw a small white hand gently touching the glass.

I turned right at the fork in the road and walked past several occupied homes. These people had survived the worst of the Trippers and were doing well on their own. They had fenced their yards with timber taken from abandoned homes and used their neighbors' land for additional grazing and planting. If you found yourself alone with five homes around you empty, you could easily gain an additional acre or three with just a few removals of fence between the yards. That's how we gained the land for our horse and our gardening.

At the end of the block, I stepped up to a gate and peeked over the top. I was at the Simpsons, a decent sized ranch house on a corner lot. They worked pretty hard to keep their land up, but while they were good farmers, they couldn't keep up in the meat. It was sad, really. They had a decent bit of forest behind them, and a small creek as well. They could have dammed that creek and had fish for the taking, and good snares would catch the small animals coming to drink. Heck, even bigger game might stroll down just for the asking to drink at the pond.

I rang the little bell that hung on a string by the gate. I knew better than to just stroll up to a house unannounced. That would get me killed or seriously hurt. Dad said back in the day a lot of people were killed by Trippers coming up to the house and people stepping out to meet them thinking they were just other folks. You learned too late that you were about to be wiped out.

"Who's out there?" a small voice called out.

I recognized Lucy's voice. Lucy Simpson was a girl about my age, and she came over to our house three days a week for schooling. She was nice, but lately she had been getting moody, and two days out the three she was mad at me or Trey for something we said or did.

"It's Josh Andrews, Lucy!" I called. "Got a rabbit for you if you want it. I got lucky on the trap line today. Mom said to bring it over to see if you wanted it."

"Leave it there," Lucy said. "Mom's not feeling well, and I don't want you to get sick."

I winced. Sickness was a constant problem, and I tended to think more people died from the flu each year than Tripper attacks.

"Will do. Hope your mom feels better soon," I said, hanging the sack over the gate.

"Thanks. Tell your mom we said thanks," Lucy said, closing the door.

I turned away, not answering, since she wouldn't have heard me anyway. I guess I got lucky in that she didn't hate me today.

I turned away, and looking down the road to the left, I could see several dark homes down a very dark road. The trees were thick, and their canopy cast deep shadows over most of the area. It nearly looked like I was standing at the entrance to a cave. I did a bit of mental calculation, and I realized this road would take me behind Trey's house which land I could cross and get to my own house quicker than backtracking the way I had come.

That sounded like a plan to me, so I moved in that direction. The sun was heading towards evening, and the adjusted sunlight lit up the entrance to the 'cave.' I seriously doubted I would have gone if it was darker, but right now it didn't seem so bad. As I walked further, I chuckled to myself, realizing I was barely a quarter mile from my house, and I could have saved myself a walk if I had only realized this route earlier.

I passed a house on the left, and it looked like it had been abandoned a long time ago. The drapes were falling down in one window, and an upper window was broken. The front door looked like it was slightly open, but I wasn't planning on going in there. The house was dead, and likely everyone who had ever lived there was dead, too.

On my right was another house, and it looked in better shape, although I doubted anyone lived there. It aroused my curiosity, because it's backyard was directly across from the backyard of the little house in the valley.

"You're a fool; go home," I told myself as I walked up the driveway. Common sense didn't win the argument, and I told myself I was just looking for information to give my dad. I looped my bow over my shoulder and put my arrow back in its quiver.

I walked up the driveway, and a squirrel chattered at me from the oak tree in the front yard. The grass was hugely overgrown and was nearly as tall as myself. The house was dark and silent, and I began to think I was the only visitor this place had had in years. In the back yard the growth was about the same, although the rose bushes were huge, out of control thorny riots of red, white, and pink. A small swing set stood lonely in the corner of the lot, and a plastic turtle graced the yard next to the cracked and weathered porch.

I looked back at the house, and it was as dark in the back as it was in the front. The house was simple but nice, and the trees around the lot meant that this place must have been nice and cool in the summer.

The back yard was fenced in, and I was grateful for the chance to get close to the creepy house without being observed. I didn't have any real reason to be doing what I was, and if I thought about it long enough, I might come up with an explanation which might have raised an excuse even for me.

At the edge of the yard, I looked at the fence for a moment. It was eight feet tall, and that was three feet higher than I was currently occupying. Hmm.

A quick glance around the yard didn't give me any inspiration, so I was about to leave when I noticed the swing set was just a foot taller than the fence. Worked for me. I climbed the play area quickly, and found myself in a small clubhouse with the roof high above me. I tried to see what was in the house, but I couldn't get a good angle on it. I worked my way to the outside of the little clubhouse, and climbed slowly to the top of the awning supports. I straddled the top beam of the clubhouse and looked out over the yard to the house beyond.

It was as every bit as dark as the front. A small stream worked its way through the properties in this area, and I could see it was deep enough to dam if they wanted a supply of water and fish right outside of their door. A big bay window allowed me to peek into the interior of the house and look around. At the worst, I could see if there was anyone living there at all that my Dad could visit.

From my perch I could see very little. It was dark and gloomy, and there didn't seem to be anyone around. The house was very neat, and there didn't seem to be a speck of dirt anywhere.

That last thought struck me as odd. Shouldn't there be some dust? Just as I pondered that, a face appeared in the far window. I was so startled I nearly fell off the swing set. As it was, I managed to nock an arrow and aim a shaft at the face staring out at me.

As quickly as It had appeared, it was gone. I wondered for a minute while I composed myself. I was breathing hard, trying to decide if I had seen a ghost. Just for the heck of it, I aimed the arrow at the house and let go, not caring where it hit. I lowered the bow, and as I climbed out of the playset, I heard a bang as the arrow I shot collided with something sturdy. I had a lot to tell Trey, and the sooner the better.

I ran back to the street and down to the cul-de-sac. One of the homes was occupied, and I could see people moving about as the day was coming to a close. I worked my way over to the back of the furthest house, guessing Trey's would be right on the line.

I checked the area and didn't see any problems, so I slipped down the bank of the creek and worked my way slowly across. I didn't mind getting wet; I knew I was going to be home soon and would be able to dry off quickly. Dad might wonder what took me so long, but he'd forget about it as soon as I told him the valley house was occupied.

On the other side of the creek I had to be wary of Trey's nets and trap lines, and it took me a good ten minutes just to clear his yard. Crossing the road, I went through the front gate of my own property and stopped cold. In the middle of the yard sticking out of the ground was my arrow—the one I had shot at the valley house. I didn't know what to do. I was panicky, because I didn't want my dad to find out, and I really didn't want my mom to find out.

I raced to the garage and put away my gear, dripping water all over the floor. Judy, dad's mare, looked at me with big brown reproachful eyes as I stumbled and dropped things all over the place. I threw an extra handful of grass in her bin to keep her quiet, and then I went back out to the yard.

The arrow was still there sticking accusingly in the lawn. I ran over to it and removed it, pulling up a good chunk of dirt. The broad head dripped soil, and as I looked it over I was struck by another surprise.

This wasn't my arrow.

CHAPTER 5

I thought about that arrow a lot over the next couple of days. I didn't tell my dad or mom about it just yet, I was afraid dad might be mad at me, and I knew mom just wouldn't understand. Besides, Dad was busy dealing with a Tripper outbreak down south of us, and he said before he left that they probably accounted for the two that had shown up the other day.

I didn't think that the occupants of the house would know where I lived unless they had followed me. That didn't make sense, as I was a pretty good stalker, and I figured I would know if someone was sneaking around in my area. I settled on the notion that they must have seen Trey and me as we stalked frogs in the creek a time or two and put two and three together to come up with my yard.

I was busy for a time, as Mom was getting back into teaching me things other than math. I was pretty well learned for my age since all my learning came from heavy reading material, not the so-called age-appropriate stuff other kids were picking up. Trey came over these days to learn as well since his mother wasn't as good at history or reading as she was at numbers. It was the only time I ever saw Mom not worry or look out the windows in fear. She buried herself in the lessons, bringing them to life and telling stories the likes of which I am sure most kids never saw. Before I was ten years old I knew about Shakespeare and Steinbeck, Dickenson and Emerson. I liked *Leaves of Grass* well enough, but I wished he would have gotten to the point about a hundred pages earlier. Walt Whitman was another long-winded soul.

Thanks to his mother's genes, Trey was a hand at math, whereas my skills tended to drift more towards the mechanical. I could figure out most things if I broke them down into easy to bite chunks. Trey just breezed through as if he were taking a stroll, which made things more difficult for me since I was constantly on the prowl for more books and materials, as ordered by my mother.

It was about noon, and we had just finished lunch when Mom announced we were running low on some supplies, especially meat. I took the hint and went out to the garage with Trey right behind me.

I took my bow off the rack and strung it, slipping my quiver over my shoulder. Trey looked at me funny.

"What are you doing?" he asked, eyeballing my gear.

"Mom wants meat; I'm getting her meat. I figure we're good for a deer or two this time of year," I said, belting on my knife. It was a simple blade with a slow, sweeping edge leading to a drop point. The seven-inch blade was a bit big for me I always thought, but Dad said it was just the right length. He never elaborated on the right length for what, but my imagination was full of unpleasant things.

Trey looked shocked, then looked over his shoulder. "Are you nuts? We've never gone out for big game without our dads before."

I shrugged. "Meat is meat. I'd rather skin one animal and get a lot of meat than ten and get just a little. Besides," I added, "you don't have to come with."

Trey frowned. "Of course I'm coming. Think I want to tell my folks I passed on a chance at deer meat?"

"Let's get moving then." I poked my head through the door just enough for my mom to see my noggin and nothing else. "Mom? Trey and I are going to check the lines for that meat you wanted."

"All right, sweetheart. Please be careful." Mom barely looked up from her book, giving me the opportunity to slip away without answering a lot of questions. Trey and I went around to the front of the house and quickly ran to his. We passed through the stone walls which bordered our properties, and I waited outside while Trey got his own gear. Trey had a crossbow which his dad had found years ago. It fired smaller arrows than my recurve, but they were just as deadly. The hardest part was finding them if Trey missed.

I had a full quiver, having spent several hours over the last two days making more arrows. It was easy to feel confident with a full arsenal, and I guess we weren't taking things too seriously as we walked down the road. We wanted to take the St. Andrews entrance since it was easier to slip through than the other areas.

As we passed the house in the small valley, I slowed and carefully inspected the dark windows. Trey slowed with me, and we moved past purposefully and deliberately.

"Man, that place gives me the creeps," Trey said. "Wonder if the stories are true."

I shook my head. "Someone lives there still. I saw them."

Trey stopped in his tracks to stare at me. I looked at him for a minute, then told him the story of how I went to the Simpson's, and then worked my way back around the house. I even told him the part about the arrow I fired and then finding it in my yard.

I don't know what I expected, but the last thing I thought Trey would do on hearing my story was to laugh at me. I waited until he calmed himself then asked him what the hell was so funny.

"Oh, I wish I could have seen it! Oh, baby, I wish I could have seen your face!" Trey just laughed some more.

"All right, I'll ask. Why?" I was getting irritated at this point and wanted to thump him on the head.

Trey straightened and looked me dead in the eye. "I put that arrow in your yard, you dope. I found it at my house and used my bow to launch it over to your place. The one you shot at the creepy house is probably still stuck in there somewhere."

Well, what the hey? I was stuck between being relieved and being sore. I settled on disturbed.

"What are you thinking, shooting arrows at my house? I ought to pound you" I snarled at Trey, not really meaning it, but trying to save some of my dignity.

Trey giggled as he held up his hands. "Oh, sure. I'll never do it again, never, never, never."

CHAPTER 6

I was about to retort when we crossed the Highland Road junction. Ordinarily we just walk, but then Lucy Simpson isn't running like crazy towards us.

"Trey! Josh! Help! There's two of them at my house! They're trying to get in!" Lucy was breathless from running, so it took a minute to get the story out. She was in the garden when two Trippers showed up, stumbling through the back lots and bouncing round the abandoned swimming pools. Lucy saw them in time and hid in the corn stalks, waiting for them to go by. As luck would have it, her brother chose that moment to open the back door and yell out for Lucy to hurry up. He barely got the door closed in time. Lucy waited for them to be distracted, then bolted.

Trey asked the obvious question. "Where's your weapon?"

Lucy pouted. "It was in the house. I was twenty yards from my door."

Trey shook his head. "There's only one at your house, by the way."

"What? No, there's two." Lucy argued.

I stepped in. "No, he's right. There's only one. The other one followed you here."

Lucy spun around and seemed to shrink into herself as she saw the Tripper stumbling towards us. It was having a hard time since the terrain was uneven, but it was coming, no doubt about it. Trippers travel in a straight line to whatever they are chasing. They don't deviate at all. They'll turn, but they won't pay attention to the terrain. Lots of them have fallen down stairs that way.

The Tripper fell into a ditch and then climbed out, its eyes fixated on us. Its mouth moved in silent rage as it worked through its diseased brain how to dismember us. It was a young woman, probably in her twenties by the look of her. She didn't seem to have that old look about her, so if I had to guess, she was infected recently. Dad would want to know about her.

Trey hefted his crossbow, and I nocked an arrow.

"What do you want to do?" he asked, his eyes narrowing.

I knew Trey was scared, but then so was I. We'd seen these things all of our lives, but that didn't mean they still didn't scare the crap out of us. We'd seen what they could do, and no one wanted to go out that way.

"Let's let her get closer, then you put one in her. I'll take a shot while you reload, deal?" I said, pulling back on my arrow.

Trey didn't bother to respond. The Tripper caught her footing and moved quickly towards us, her eyes wide and furious. The splotches on her face were bright red, and stood out angrily against her pale skin. Trey aimed quickly and let fly, the bolt whipping through the air. It struck her throat with a deep smack, causing her to stumble and grab at her neck. When her hands reached the shaft, she began pulling the bolt out, tearing and stretching her skin. She finally wrenched the thing out, and started for us again.

It was hard to focus considering there was a large bloody hole in the middle of the Tripper's throat which blew bubbles of blood for every breath she exhaled. I didn't have a lot of choice, now that gaping wound was a serious risk to all of us, and her bloody hands would be brimming with infection.

I lined up my shot on her head, which was easier since she was a lot closer now. I could see Trey working quickly with his crossbow, but he would never have that bolt loaded in time. Lucy was stepping back, and I imagine she was looking for a place to run to.

I waited another heartbeat then let go of my bow string. My arrow struck the woman in the bridge of her nose, into her eye, and punched through the fragile bones of the eye socket. She collapsed without another step forward.

I released the breath I was holding, and looking back at Lucy, I noticed she was further away than I figured. I wondered briefly if she was just about to cut and run and let Trey and me handle this alone. That thought didn't sit well with me, but I decided not to bring it up.

"Nice shot," Trey said, walking over to the dead woman.

"I'm getting a lot of practice these days," I said. At Trey's look I quickly related the story of the man I shot over by the place where we had killed the other.

Trey looked around. "What's going on, man? We don't see a Tripper for months, maybe a year, then we see three in just a couple of days? Ain't right, man."

"I know. Let's get our arrows," I said. My dad would kill me if he knew what I was doing, but I really hated making new arrows. Everything was easy except for the stupid fletching. One would always be off center, then I'd have to start over.

Trey had it easy. He just picked his up off the ground. He wiped it off on the woman's leg, leaving long streaks of red on her thigh. I had to brace my foot on the woman's face, and it was a little uncomfortable yanking out the arrow from one eye while the other looked at me. Lucky for me though, the wound was tight, and there was little residue left on the arrow. I wasn't fooled, though. I knew there was a lot of virus on that head and shaft. I took out a lighter and quickly burned the areas that had been touched by the virus. Handing it over to Trey, he did the same with his bolt. Dad said it was the best way to kill the virus since nothing could survive open flames.

I put the now-blackened arrow back into my bow and started forward. Trey looked at me funny.

"Hey, man, the woods are that way," he said, pointing to the south.

"Yeah, but there's another Tripper at Lucy's house, remember?" I replied. I didn't look back to see if Lucy was following, and at the moment I really didn't care. Suddenly, I got mad about the whole thing. I turned around and started walking back towards the entrance to the subdivision. Trey spun around and followed.

"What are you doing?" he asked, looking back at Lucy who seemed shocked as hell that I was leaving a Tripper at her house unattended.

"Tripper at the Simpson's is none of my business," I said, walking on.

Lucy stopped suddenly. "What?" she shouted. "What the hell?"

I turned around and looked at her. "You and your family survived just like we did when the Tripper mobs came over the land. I think your family can handle one. Besides," I added, "I'm not going to risk my neck by being mistaken for another Tripper by poking around your place where the family is a little jumpy right now, hey?"

Well, that knocked them both back a peg, and neither of them had anything to say to me at that point. I figured logic won over emotion, and Trey proved it by shrugging his shoulders and falling in line with me on our way to the hunting grounds.

Lucy just stood there for a minute, then it seemed like family duty called, and she started heading back to her house. I figured she'd be okay since there was only one Tripper and there were several fully grown adult males at her place. In all likelihood, she'd arrive just in time for cleanup.

CHAPTER 7

Trey and I walked over the road to the woods and slipped in pretty easily. We'd been in here hundreds of times, and our trap lines were just to the east of us. We'd check them when we got back, assuming we had any luck whatsoever in our hunt.

The brush was thick, but we'd made trails through here before. The trees were only about twenty years old, to hear my dad talk about it, and so there was a lot of space between the bigger trees. A little to the south was a more formidable tree line, and Trey and I headed right for it. The deer we were looking for wouldn't be in this area, but if we headed further west, we might get luckier.

"Creek is down," Trey said as we jumped over a foot-wide stream that wound its way through the woods. The banks of the creek were steep, and if they ever filled, we'd see three-foot deep creeks that were about ten feet wide. We'd never get across without help if that happened.

"Good for us to cross, bad for us to find meat," I said, swinging on a branch. We crossed the creek and worked our way south, trying to see if there were any tracks worth a look.

Trey was the better tracker between the two of us, and I wasn't about to argue the point. I could track something well enough, but Trey had a knack for figuring out where the game went. He seemed to read the land differently than me, and I didn't stand in his way. I figured he'd get us meat, and the best I could do was shut up and follow along.

After circling a bit, Trey settled into a line and followed it for a few feet, then it went off in another direction. He followed that one for a time, then went another way. He was so focused on reading signs that he completely missed the fact that we had left the woods and were nearly at another road.

"Trey!" I called, spooking any game nearby.

"What? What's the...oh." Trey looked around and saw we were well out of the woods. It didn't take a genius to figure out that any large game would have spotted us easily by now and were long gone.

"C'mon, let's head west," I said, walking at the bottom of the ditch that paralleled the road.

Trey nodded and fell in behind me, his crossbow slung over his back like my recurve. I held onto the arrow that had killed that infected woman since I didn't want to put it in my quiver, and every once in a while I would use it to hack down a particularly large weed. We passed an old church on our right and then a couple of schools. Dad said a lot of people died in those buildings thinking they would be good places to fort up against the Trippers. Problem was, the people inside didn't get along, and it all fell apart. Rumor had it the places were haunted, and if you were around at night you could hear voices and see lights go on and off. I never stuck around for the show, thank you very much.

"Think there's anything in those buildings we could use?" Trey said, somehow reading into what I was thinking.

I shook my head. "Doubt it. What would be left?"

"I don't know. Let's go take a look!" Trey said, leaving the ditch and walking across a small field. An unusually shaped fence sat sentry in a corner, and Trey walked around it carefully. It was shaped like a quarter of a sphere, and I couldn't imagine for the life of me what it was intended to keep in or out.

"Trey! We have hunting to do! Come on!" I shouted, trying to get him back on track.

"If you're scared, stay there. I'll come back for you later," Trey taunted.

Well, that did it. Trey knew there was no way I was going to let him go somewhere and claim I was too scared, so I pulled my bow off my shoulder and nocked the arrow I was holding. I don't know why I did it, I just felt better for doing it.

Trey watched me with an amused grin on his face, and if I were so inclined, I might have smacked him for it. But we tripped onto a sidewalk very quickly, and our banter became silent as we approached the big buildings.

In reality, there were two schools here, joined by a long connecting section. I had seen the buildings before, but always from a distance, and I never had the urge to go see what was inside.

The front of the building closest to us was kind of scary. The entrance was under an overhang which darkened everything. The sides of the entrance came out about twenty yards, and they curved slightly inward, like they were going to drag you in if you came to close. I didn't like the look of it at all, but Trey was not to be denied.

"Look, there's a place we can get in." He pointed to a large section of glass that had been broken which was a bottom panel of a door. It wasn't completely broken through, so no animals or anything else had been through there.

"Maybe we should try the doors first before we go crawling through glass," I suggested with just a touch of sarcasm.

"Picky, picky," Trey said. But that didn't stop him from trying the doors.

I took extreme satisfaction from the fact that the door he was going to crawl through actually opened when he pulled on it.

Trey held the door open. "After you," he said.

"Oh, no. This was your idea. You go first," I insisted.

Trey shot me a withering look. "Baby."

"What was that line mom taught us about fools?" I asked innocently.

Trey frowned as he got my point. He checked his crossbow and slowly walked through the door. I was a good two steps behind him, and that was just so I didn't accidentally poke him with my possibly poisoned arrow.

The front part of the building was clear although there were some papers on the floor. To our left was an area that looked like an office, and my suspicions were confirmed when I saw a sign on the door that read 'Office'.

I didn't see anything of interest in there, so I just shook my head at Trey who walked down a small hallway that passed in front of the office. We crossed an opening that looked like it led into a large area, but it was very dark and not very inviting. We could see across the opening thanks to light coming in from another hallway in the back, but it was still pretty dark.

Trey kept moving down the hall, and he stopped in front of a door. If I had to guess, it went into a classroom, but it wasn't easy to tell. Trey tried the handle, and it was locked. There were dark stains all over the place down here, and I couldn't think of anything good that could cause such stains.

"Let's try the other side," Trey said quietly.

I didn't say anything, I just shrugged. This was Trey's show, and I wasn't going to jump in anywhere.

We walked back across the office and over to the other side of the foyer. There was a larger opening on this side, and it also led to the very dark area in the middle of the school. Trey walked along the wall while I circled wide. My dad had always taught us to spread out as much as we could when we were hunting anything, and I figured it was as appropriate here as it was in the woods.

The area in front of us was dark, but there was nothing in it except for a bunch of benches and tables. If I had to guess, I'd say this was where everyone came to eat when they were here. There were more papers and garbage on the floor, but nothing of interest.

"What's in there?" Trey asked. He pointed behind me to the big set of double doors I didn't know I was standing in front of.

"Beats me. Help yourself," I said, stepping away from the big doors.

"Dang, you gonna make me do all the work?" Trey said, frowning.

"*You* wanted to come in here to see what was what, *you* can see what is what," I said, sounding somewhat stupid.

Trey shook his head and pulled on the handles. Neither of them worked, so we walked along the wall until we came across another set of double doors. These didn't work either, and I was beginning to figure we weren't going to get in. The last set of doors opened, but only slightly. We could barely make out that they had been chained together on the other side.

"Well, that tells us one thing," Trey said.

"Do tell," I prompted, looking around at a huge eating room which seemed to be big enough to have a stage on it.

"There might be some stuff worth recovering if no one else has been able to get in there," Trey said.

I tossed that around in my head for a second. "Maybe it's full of sleeping Trippers, too."

CHAPTER 8

Trey just shook his head and moved down a very dark hallway. It was dark enough that we stopped for a minute and pulled a candle out of his pack. I had the lighter, so we lit the candle, throwing weak but welcome light into our area.

As it turned out, we were standing next to a flight of stairs that would take us to the second floor. Trey didn't even ask before he started up the steps. I had to follow since he was carrying the candle.

The second floor, as it turned out, wasn't as scary as the first. There was a lot of light coming in from the huge windows at the end of the hallways, and there were a few skylights that helped a great deal.

Trey looked in the first room we came to and shook his head. I walked over to the other side of the hallway and checked a room on that side. It was cleared of anything useful as well. I don't know who we were kidding. Unless it came up to us and told us what it would be useful for, we wouldn't really know it. I told Trey the same thing.

"You never know," Trey said. "That's what my Daddy always says. You never know."

"You may be right about that," I said as I ducked into a room. Trey waited in the hallway, and I popped out quickly, showing him my prizes.

"I'll be damned. You looking to make points with your Mom, or what?"

I grinned. I had pulled out a couple of history textbooks, but I couldn't be sure of the grade level. In any case, Trey and I had something other than the books my mom had scrounged up for teaching. I think I may have helped our education by leaps and bounds, not to mention our attention spans.

The next rooms in the hallway didn't have anything of worth, and I was thinking we were wasting hunting time when we crossed over to the other side. Right away we could tell things were different. There was a feel to the air that wasn't there before, and the big windows on the end of the hallways were covered up with big drapes. They almost looked like bedsheets.

"Something's not right there, bro," Trey said.

I nodded my head in agreement. Since I didn't have to hold the candle, I kept both hands on my bow, ready to fire at a second's notice.

"Let's get that sheet off; see what we can see," Trey whispered.

I personally thought that was not the greatest idea because I wasn't sure I wanted to see what I could see. But I walked carefully over to the sheet and gave it a yank. The sudden brightness blinded us for a second, and when we could see, it wasn't a good thing.

The Trippers had been here, no doubt about it. There were a lot of dark stains all over the floor, and bloody handprints streaked the walls and doors. There was a strange smell in the stale air, and the candle was burning slightly brighter for some reason.

"I don't like the looks of this," Trey said, walking slowly down the hall.

"Little late, don't you think?" I said, bringing my bow forward and adjusting my fingers on the string.

"Let's just check a couple rooms, and get out of here." Trey said.

I personally thought that wasn't a better idea than walking around this hallway, but what did I know?

Trey went to a room and tried the door. The handle moved easily, and we took a look inside, gagging a little from the stench that greeted us at the door. The room was decently lit since the window was uncovered, and I really wished it hadn't been.

There were four people still in that room, and they looked terrible. There was a young man in a curled up position near the door, and he almost looked like he was sleeping except for the huge dark stain under his head and shoulders. If we pushed him over, I'd bet my bow his throat had been torn out.

Another body was on the ground, and this one was even more gruesome than the last. Its stomach had been torn open, and the guts had been thrown all over. Ropes of intestine hung from the desks and chairs, and something that looked like a liver was off to one side.

Two more small bodies were on the ground, and they looked like they hadn't been torn open, but rather had their heads bashed in on one of the desks.

I couldn't help myself. "Gee, wonder what the next room is like?"

Trey backed away with me and didn't say a word. We had seen what Trippers could do when the rage was on them, and this was nothing new. I'd never seen it so up close before, and it was weirdly fascinating.

"I think we're done up here. Even if there was something here, I don't want to get it. We'll let our dads know after we finish hunting," he said.

I wondered about that. I wasn't sure I wanted to tell my father about our little trip. I don't think he would have approved.

Trey led the way, and we backtracked the way we had come. It was a relief to get back downstairs and get away from the smell and the feel of death all over the place. Trey turned left when he exited the big double doors and headed down a long hallway which I thought took us east, but I was slightly turned around.

The hallway was nearly without doors or windows, but there was a single door to the north as we ventured further into the gloom. Trey put a hand on it and looked back at me.

I shook my head, figuring there was nothing here worth keeping, so just leave it alone. Trey silently agreed, and we moved on.

About one hundred yards down the hallway, we found another set of double doors. By this time, I had figured out where we were and what it as we were standing in front of.

"It's a side door to the gym," I said.

"How do you know?"

"Because the name on the side says 'GYM'." I said, trying out my new sarcasm.

Trey wisely avoided the trap and pulled on the door handle. It wasn't very dark here since we were close to a side door, but since we didn't know what was in the gym, we kept the candle lit.

I stood off to the side, drawing my string back. If there was something on the other side of the door, I'd rather greet it with an arrow than my face.

Trey peeked around as the door slowly closed and stopped it with his hand before it shut. "Looks okay. Let's take a quick look inside."

I followed and we stepped into the gloom. The candle was not very bright, but it threw shadows and light all over the place. Trey held it high, and the light of the candle was barely able to get to the ceiling, and we could make out some dark opening at the other end of the room. Right next to us was a small hallway with a sign that said 'GIRLS LOCKER ROOM".

Over by a tall wooden structure was a pile of clothing and supplies. When I stepped over that way, my foot struck something. It felt soft and stiff at the same time, and I really didn't want to look down. As a matter of fact, I was doing everything I could, apart from closing my eyes, to *not* look down.

"Trey?"

"What?"

"What's on the floor?"

"Hang on."

I saw the light shift as Trey brought the candle to the floor. My eyes had adjusted to the gloom, and I could see very clearly the body at my feet. I could also see the bodies all over the floor. They were everywhere, lying in various positions. Some were on their backs; others were in little balls. Some were face down and tucked in corners that were the made at the bottom of the wooden wall. The floor was dark and heavily stained in dried blood. The bodies were mostly dried-out husks with sunken cheeks and exposed bones. Several seemed almost normal, and they looked weird to me.

"Holy crap," Trey said.

"Yeah."

"Wonder why those ones are in better shape than the rest?" Trey wondered out loud.

I didn't answer because I didn't have to. Three of the corpses heads turned, and their eyes opened at the same time. There was a hesitation as they figured out what we were, and then they were slowly trying to get to their feet.

CHAPTER 9

"Go. Now," I said, turning and running for the door. Trey was right behind me. The candlelight was coming from behind and below, having been dropped by Trey. We cast huge shadows onto the wall as we bolted for the exit. Behind us, the Trippers we had awakened were remembering how to walk, and were gaining ground.

"Go, go!" Trey yelled as we hit the door. Thankfully, they opened outward, so we could just bolt through without stopping.

"Which way?" I shouted as we made the hallway.

"Outside, just go!" Trey yelled, bolting for the exit.

"Move, OW!" I stopped suddenly as pain exploded in my face.

"What the hell?" Trey yelled.

"Just go, go!" I said, rubbing my injured forehead.

We ran to the big exit doors and had to stop again. The doors were held together with some serious-looking chains, and we had no way of even trying to find the key to the big brass padlock that stopped us cold.

Behind us, the gym door banged as the Trippers ran into it, and it was only a matter of time before they found their way out.

I exhaled and adjusted my stance, angling my bow for a smooth draw. I was reaching into my quiver for a second arrow when Trey stopped me.

"Come on! We can get out!" he said excitedly as he pointed to the doors.

Trey pushed on the big doors, and there was enough slack in the chain to let a couple of skinny kids squeeze through the opening. I nodded and set my bow aside as Trey put his crossbow down. I pushed on the doors, holding them open while Trey wiggled through the narrow opening. On the other side, he held the doors open as I passed.through the bows.

I was just about to start going through when Trey suddenly yelled.

"Move your ass! They're right behind you!"

I didn't bother to look, mostly because I didn't want to. If I looked, I would freeze. If I froze, I was dead. I threw myself at the opening as Trey held it, wiggling as fast as I could between this legs.

"Hurry, hurry, *JESUS!*" Trey fell back as the doors began to close. Dark hands slammed into the doors, opening them slightly again, just enough for a Tripper hand to slip through and grasp my pant leg.

"TREY! It's got my leg!" I shrieked, trying to crawl away from the nasty hand that gripped my pants. My efforts pulled the arm of the Tripper through the opening, and the infected person raised its dark eyes to me and hissed loudly.

Trey grabbed me by my armpits and tried to move me backwards, but the Tripper held on. It started to pull me back, and the other two Trippers were pushing on the door now, too, adding their snarls and snaps to the jingling sound of the straining chains.

Trey held on to me but tried to reach his crossbow at the same time. It was two feet out of reach, and useless as a daisy at the moment.

"Rush the door on this side!" I yelled in a moment of desperate inspiration.

"What? Are you nuts?" Trey asked.

"*Just do it!*" I yelled.

Trey let go, and immediately I could feel myself being dragged back to the building. If I came within biting range, it was all over.

"*Hurry!*"

Trey took a step back, then launched himself at the door, colliding with it and knocking back one of the Trippers. The one on the ground, the one that had me, looked up and tried to reach through the glass to get at Trey.

"Again! I think she loosened her grip!" I yelled, as I tried to find something to hold on to as the Tripper dragged me closer and closer.

Trey stepped further back and flew at the metal part of the door, slamming into it with all of his strength. The Tripper holding me suddenly released her grip, having had her arm broken in the door frame. She never winced, she just stood up slowly and joined her brother and sister in staring out the window at the two of us.

They pushed on the doors, so the opening was still there, and we could easily kill all three if we had to. I retrieved my bow when Trey stopped me.

"This just is not our day." He pointed to the east, and I nearly just ran away.

A lone Tripper was barreling down at us, and would be on top of us if Trey hadn't pointed it out,

I didn't even aim, I just brought my bow up and fired. The arrow punched into the Tripper's chest, and he slowed down to look at the stick coming out of his chest. He looked up at us with his glazed eyes, and tried to run again, but he slowed and fell to his knees. I had another arrow nocked and ready, and Trey was aiming his crossbow at the man, but even he hesitated.

The Tripper grabbed feebly at the arrow, but his face contorted, and he seemed to shrink in on himself as he fell to the side. He closed his eyes and he just lay there. After a minute, he slowly relaxed and straightened slightly.

"What the hell?" Trey asked out loud.

I was thinking the same thing. You weren't supposed to be able to stop them by shooting them in the chest. At least, none of the ones I've seen my father shoot like that ever did. Weird.

"Do you think it's really dead?" I asked, moving forward cautiously.

Trey shrugged. "Never knew one to stop coming once it saw something it wanted to kill."

"Is it dead or did I trigger a sleep?" I was genuinely curious, because I had never seen such a thing before.

"Feel free to give it a poke," Trey said. "I'll cover you."

I shrugged and reached out with my bow. I tapped it on the arm and then the head. I finally poked it in the eye, and none of that provoked any kind of response.

"Guess it's dead," I said. "Definitely need to tell dad about this one."

"Let's get out of here," Trey said.

"Fine, but just to be clear, this was your idea."

"Thanks."

CHAPTER 10

We went back to the road we had been following and walked past a small park area. My dad told me in the old days, families would come out here and sit and have lunch. They would let their kids run through the park and have a good time. When the Trippers came, that ended pretty quick. Now the equipment was rusted and falling apart. The wooden towers were home to birds and animals and would probably fall over in the next wind storm.

About a mile later, we left the road and headed into the woods. There was a good sized forest here about twice the size of the one we got most of our game in. This one promised to have larger game like deer. Trey and I spread out, stepping through the underbrush and trying not to break any twigs or branches.

I kept my bow low with my right arm across my chest. I could bring up the bow and fire in a split second, having been taught that by my father. My aiming was more instinctual than actual, as Dad called it. I had no real idea what he was talking about, all I knew was the arrows went where I wanted them to, or pretty close to it.

A low whistle reached my ears, and I looked over at Trey to see him wave a hand forward. I looked and saw a decent sized doe making her way slowly through the trees. She hadn't winded us yet, so we waited silently. If her path stayed true, she would pass within ten feet of Trey. If her path stayed true, and Trey released his arrow at the right time, I was in danger of being on the receiving end if he missed.

Great. I signaled to Trey for him to take the doe, and I carefully slipped back around a tree, positioning it between myself and Trey. I brought my bow up slowly and waited, not pulling back on the string just yet.

I could hear the doe moving through the leaves, and I knew Trey was waiting for the best shot which was when she just began to walk away from him. A crossbow wasn't the worst thing to kill a deer with, but Trey had proven to be a rotten shot with a longbow.

I heard a slap, like someone had hit themselves in the leg, and suddenly the forest was full of sound as the doe jumped forward. I stepped out with my bow at full draw, and let fly as the animal leapt past. A second slap and the doe stumbled, running forward another twenty yards before falling to the ground.

Trey and I moved forward slowly, not letting the deer see us. We didn't want her to get up and run off, further away this time. That was another thing Dad had taught me. Never work harder than you have to when it comes to hunting.

After a minute the doe was still, and another minute later she was dead. Trey and I moved up and inspected our kill.

"Nice shot," I said, noting his bolt was deep in the deer's chest.

"Yours, too." Trey pointed at my arrow which was sticking out of the deer's neck, right underneath the jaw.

"Well, let's get to it. Right side or left?" I said, drawing my knife.

"Left," Trey said, plunging his knife into the deer's haunch.

"All yours."

Half an hour later we were trudging back home, each of us lugging a leg of deer over our shoulder. It was awkward as hell, but we managed it. We didn't say anything as we went past the old school, and we could see the three Trippers we had left there still at the door, still pushing on the chain. I made a mental note to tell my father about them before any other fool kid wandered into the school.

When I got home, my Dad was already there, so I figured there wasn't any time like now to spread the news.

"Hey, son. Nice bit of meat you have there. Did Trey get some?" Dad asked.

"He got the left side. Dad?" I hesitated.

My father looked at me and put down the comb he was using on his horse Judy. "What is it?"

"Trey and I went into the old school up the way" I said quietly.

My father's eyes narrowed slightly. But he stayed silent and let me speak.

"We didn't find anything of value, but we woke up three Trippers. One of them almost got me." I told him about our trip and narrow escape, and the one we killed out in the school grounds. Dad's eyes got wider at that part.

"Wait. Back up. What happened to the Tripper in the yard?" he asked.

"I shot it in the chest, and it died," I said, telling him how the man had curled up and stopped moving.

"Interesting." Dad was silent for a moment. "I wonder if that explains..." He wandered off for a second before focusing back on me. "Well, that makes three. The two by the dam, and the one by the school."

"Four," I said, looking down again.

"What?"

"Trey and I killed another before we headed out. It's over by the Simpsons. Probably another by their house as well."

"Jesus Christ. All right, that does it. Five in four days is way over the limit. You are confined to the house and yard until I sort this out. I'm going to talk to Trey's dad and get Trey's story from him."

"How long?" I asked, contemplating a whole lot of school and chores.

"Until I say different, Joshua. You've handled yourself better than I could have ever hoped for. But what would you have done had you gotten bit? You're a big boy, but Trippers are adults fueled by fear and rage. You can't fight one off, and I realize I should have started your other training years ago," Dad said kindly. "I'm not mad at you, but you're my only child, and every day I'm scared to death something will happen to you when I'm not there. You're a better woodsman than I am, but you can't fight Trippers. Not by yourself."

"What am I supposed to do?" I asked, not sure where this was going.

"Help your mom, make more arrows, and jerk that venison," Dad said, picking up his gun and heading out the door to go make Trey's life as miserable as mine.

Great. Just great. I had only one thing to say to all this.

"Shit."

CHAPTER 11

"Maybe it's time we faced the truth that we aren't safe here."

"What truth is that? Every major community was overrun by the Trippers. The only way we survived, the way anyone survived, was hunkering down and taking care of their own."

"Your son has been attacked three times, and you think we're safe? He should never leave the yard."

"That's crazy. How the hell is he supposed to learn any skills if he's stuck here?"

My parents had been arguing for two days, and I was getting an earful. My mom wanted us to pack up and go to a community with more than just a handful of homes hanging on to a hand-to-mouth existence. My dad was holding out, saying he had a responsibility to the people who were out on the fringe like we were. All I knew was I didn't want to leave my home; not for anything. But for the moment, I was stuck here, listening to the same argument over and over again.

Lost in my thoughts, I didn't realize the conversation had ended, and my mother was standing in my doorway.

"Time for school, Josh," Mom said, looking out the window while she spoke. My windows faced the front of the house, and I could see all the way over to Trey's house. Mom was looking to see if Trey was going to come over, but I knew he wasn't. He was as quarantined as I was after our little trip to the old school. When Trey's dad found out it was Trey's idea that nearly got us killed, I hadn't seen him since.

I swung my feet off my bed, knocking over a couple of arrows I had at the edge. Since I had nothing else to do, I was making arrows. I used pheasant feathers for fletching and cedar for the shafts. They worked, but it took some time. I had made three dozen and was waiting for the chance to go back to the woods and get more supplies.

I went downstairs and made my way into the back room. Mom had converted it into a small classroom complete with bulletin boards and bookshelves. She was writing on the chalkboard when

I got there, and I took a second to get a look at her. She was a small woman with brown hair and brown eyes. She looked tired today, and if I remembered right, she looked tired a lot. Dad said Mom had a lot of memories, and they worked together to bring her down from time to time.

Mom used to leave the house a lot, but lately all she's done is go to the garden or weed her flowerbeds.

I worried about her because she seemed too fragile, like the smallest thing could make her break. Dad said she was stronger than she looked, and I hoped so.

School was about four hours, and it was time for lunch when we finished. I learned about the Fertile Crescent and ancient Sumer. I liked history the best. It was fun to learn about where we came from. Sometimes I wondered what historians might make of this little episode in mankind's history.

Dad came home early and had lunch with us, which was a nice treat. Even Mom seemed to brighten a little when she saw Dad was home early. After lunch, I went outside to practice with my arrows, and was putting most of them in a good group across the yard when Dad came out to see what I was up to.

"Nice work, Josh," Dad said when he saw my target. "Why are you practicing at targets that are so far away?"

I shrugged. "I figured if I could hit a small circle at fifty yards, then anything closer was just that much easier."

Dad nodded slowly as he digested that. "Good thinking." He surprised me with his next sentence. "I think it's time you learned to defend yourself."

I didn't know what else to say but "Okay!" I was kind of excited to be learning a few moves to defend myself, but I was a little curious about what my dad could teach me. I never suspected that he knew anything other than how to shoot people.

We went out to the yard, and I was always curious as to what it might have looked like before the infection hit. Our yard was big with many tall trees. Dad worked hard to keep the yard looking neat and trimmed, and we had a push mower to cut the grass. The bushes around the house were trimmed to about head high (to me), and there was a shed in the back where the horse feed was kept. A tall rock fence surrounded the yard, and it cut off the rest of the world. Dad built that fence after the first wave of infected hit the area, and it's saved us a couple of times since.

"Okay. Let's see what you think you know," Dad said. "Pretend I'm a Tripper coming to get you." Dad put up his hands and started moving towards me.

I didn't know what else to do, so I ran away and hid behind a tree. I didn't hear him coming, so I peeked out to see where he was. That's when a big hand grabbed me and pulled me from my tree. I yelped as I got pulled in, and gasped when I got thrown to the ground. I figured the lesson was there, but I squawked in surprise when my dad started to pound me with his fists.

"Ow! What the...? Dad!" I curled up into a ball, covering my neck with my hands.

The pounding stopped. "You're dead, son. First lesson. Never stop moving, and never stop fighting." Dad stood up and helped me to my feet.

I rubbed my back and sides where he had hit me. I was more surprised than hurt. "What do I fight with?"

Dad smiled. "Your head."

"Huh?"

"Use your head to win a fight. Outthink your enemy. Use what you have. You're not going to win a fight with a bigger person or Tripper unless you think." Dad motioned me over to the open area. "Let's try again. And if you just curl up and fall down again, I'll hit you harder until you learn."

Let me tell you, that was a lesson I learned right then and there. We stepped out into the open, and Dad came at me again. This time I ran over to the line of bushes that separated the side yard from the back yard. I slipped underneath the branches between two of them, sliding out the other side. I could hear my dad approaching, and I ducked down, running along the bushes towards the back wall. I knew the bushes thinned out back there, and as I ran I made a plan.

Reaching the end, I moved back to the back yard, and I saw my dad trying to get through the bushes. I ran wide to stay out of his peripheral vision and came up behind him. He was about a third of the way through the bushes, growling and cursing. I threw myself at his back, shoving him deeper into the shrubbery and getting a startled "Whoa!" for my efforts.

I moved away and ran over to the house, sitting down on the back porch. I waited for my dad to pull himself out of the branches that seemed to grab him at every move.

Finally, he got out and walked over to where I sat. I smiled innocently, trying hard not to laugh at the leaf covered giant headed my way.

Dad looked at me for a long time. I looked back, knowing he was trying to figure out what to do with me.

Suddenly, we heard a noise. It was a strange choking sound, like someone was trying to breathe but just couldn't. Dad cocked his head and then went to look in the kitchen window.

"Great. I'll never hear the end of it now," he said, heading back off the porch and into the yard.

I went over to the window and looked in. On the floor, my mother was convulsed in laughter, holding her sides and rolling around. I stared for a minute since I had never seen her laugh so hard. It was a good thing to see.

"Josh! Over here! We're not done," Dad called.

I left the window, and I felt pretty good knowing I had made my mother laugh. It was at my dad's expense, but it felt good, nonetheless.

CHAPTER 12

We worked for another hour and called it quits after that. I had several bruises and a skinned knee, and dad had a bruised chin from an elbow I got in through his defense. It was an accident, but I think he was secretly proud of me for taking to his instruction as well as I had. He taught me holds and strikes and ways to leverage a larger opponent. Always he stressed thinking, outsmarting, planning.

After another two days at home, my mother finally conceded it was time to let me go out and hunt again. We were running low on meat, and the deer haunch only lasted so long. My trap lines hadn't been checked in a week, and I worried that anything caught wouldn't be fit to eat.

Workouts with my dad became routine, and every day we worked on fighting and evading. After a month, we worked with weapons. We used only knives for the most part, since that was all we had. There was a hatchet for the kindling, but Dad said to leave it.

It was around the first hint of fall that my dad decided he wanted to take me on a trip. I was excited as all get out, but Mom was worried she might not see either of us again. It took Dad another three days before he convinced her it was going to be all right. We were only going to the wall and back. That was it. Mom was going to stay with Trey's family so she wouldn't be alone, and she could keep educating Trey. I hadn't seen Trey since our little expedition, but Dad said he was fine and was working on a mountain of chores his dad had come up with.

Dad helped me pack a backpack for the trip. I had water, some jerky, and some dried fruits and nuts. I had a change of clothes, some socks, and a small first aid kit. In a small can was some matches, cotton balls, and two small candles. A length of rope finished the kit.

I put on the backpack, then took it off, looking at it critically. Dad caught me looking.

"What is it?" He asked, putting together his own pack.

"I can't wear my quiver with this on," I said.

Dad looked at the backpack. "I think we can come up with something." He took the pack and my quiver and worked on it for a little while. After an hour, he came back with a great solution. My quiver was attached to the right side of my backpack. I put the combination on and tried to get an arrow out. Instead of pulling an arrow out diagonally, I was going to have to pull it out vertically, but it worked out just the same. The arrows were roughly in the same place as they were when I just had the quiver, so it was fine.

"Works well, thanks," I said.

Dad looked at me critically. "I think you're missing something," he said. "I'll be right back." He walked off to the stairs to the basement, and I could hear him rummaging around. I couldn't think of anything I needed, so I just waited.

Dad came back with a small box. It was about a foot long and a couple of inches wide. He gave it to me with a small smile.

I opened it and had to smile myself. Inside was a beautiful knife. The blade was about seven inches long and was attached to a rough-looking white handle. The edge looked extremely sharp, and I knew from experience that it was not a toy.

"I think you've earned this," Dad said, taking the knife out of the box. The sheath was a simple leather affair, and I hurriedly slipped in on my belt. Dad put the knife where it belonged, then took a step back. "You're growing up, Josh. No denying that. I hope there's something left of the world for you when your time comes."

"What do you mean?" I asked, puzzled. I was thrilled with the gift; it was the first present my dad had given me that wasn't connected to my birthday or Christmas.

"I'll tell you later. Let's get ourselves cleaned up and ready for supper. We'll leave in the morning," Dad said, ruffling my hair.

"Okay. Thanks, by the way. I love it," I said, looking down at the knife sticking out of my belt.

Dad smiled. "I did, too, when my dad gave it to me."

I didn't know what to say to that, but by the time I had a question, Dad was already headed for supper.

CHAPTER 13

In the morning, we pulled out a couple bicycles and headed east. Dad wanted to go a little south before we went east, so we zig-zagged our way down farm roads and back country lanes. The fields were full of untended grass and crops, and homes we passed had long been abandoned and looted. Some of the homes we passed were burned out wrecks, and in some cases we could make out the distinct white of bones in the yards. It was such a contrast to the world I knew that I had to ask my dad about it.

"Dad?"

"What's up, Josh?"

"What was it like during the bad times?"

My dad thought for a minute as we pedaled away the miles. He got a faraway look in his eyes like he was seeing something in the distance that wasn't really there.

"It wasn't good, Josh. People were panicking all over. Trippers were everywhere, but they weren't the real problem. Neighbor turned against neighbor; people were killed for no reason other than they had something the other person thought they needed. Chicago was a war zone with gangs establishing kingdoms in what used to be the better parts of town. The police were so overwhelmed they were useless, and in a couple cases joined with the gangs. We weren't sure why the disease spread so far so fast. There wasn't any good information coming out, and people were just going crazy. No one was paying attention to the Trippers, and they eventually took over."

"How come they didn't just shoot them all, Dad?" I asked.

"They didn't have enough bullets, and the police had been spread so thin trying to put down the riots and the gangs that the situation just got out of control. Politicians were trying to score points against each other and blaming each other that no one stepped up lo lead. Eventually, things were just left alone, and we were on our own, every last one of us."

I couldn't understand how no one could lead. My education was full of men stepping up to do the right thing, to lead the way, and here my dad was telling me that such men didn't exist anymore.

I pedaled a bit further, then I had another question.

"Dad?"

"Yes, Josh?"

"Did the rest of the country get overrun with Trippers, too?"

"From what we understood, it was worse everywhere else than it was here. No one knows why. The east coast has a lot more people on it, so I'm sure that played a part. But the south and west should have been able to take care of things. All we knew was suddenly a lot of trucks showed up and started building the wall."

"What is the wall?" I asked. I'd heard the term before and seen pictures, but I never got the story from anyone. Trey's dad just shook his head, and mine just spoke about it briefly. I was actually excited to be going to see it.

"It was the government's last attempt to save civilization. We were the only state that still had a viable population, so they decided to shield us from the rest of the country. Nothing can get us in here. The only threat is our own Trippers, but we seem to be able to handle them." Dad reached over and tussled my hair, and we both nearly crashed when he temporarily bumped his bike into mine.

We straightened ourselves without injury and kept moving. Down the back road, we passed a group of houses that were set further back from the road than I was used to seeing. There was a huge road down the middle of the houses, and I could see each house had a great big garage attached to it.

"Lot of cars in those houses?" I asked my dad as we cycled past.

"Not cars, buddy. Planes," Dad said.

"What?"

"In that subdivision, the people there owned their own airplanes and kept them near their houses. When they wanted to go on a trip, they would move them to that big road, and fly away," Dad said, looking over the homes.

"What happened to all the people who lived there?" I asked. The community was gated and had a sturdy fence all the way around it as far as I could tell. Trippers couldn't get in if they blocked the main entrance.

"I guess they flew away when the trouble hit. At least they could, not like the rest of us." Dad got quiet, and we pedaled past the houses without incident.

We reached Manhatten-Monee road and turned left. My dad explained it would take right to the border without going south any further. I didn't care if it took us to the moon. I was thrilled to have this time to myself with my dad, something I rarely got to do. Another thing I rarely got to do was see my father in action against a Tripper. As I soon saw, today was going to be an exception.

Just past a small group of homes a lone man was walking along the road. His jerky movements told us immediately that something was wrong, and my dad motioned me to slow down and stop. Dad parked his bike without ever taking his eyes of the infected man. The man was smaller than my dad, but wider. He had a shock of yellow hair that stuck out at wild angles, giving his head the look of a sun drawn by a little kid.

Dad slipped his pack off and pulled out his axe. It was more of a camp axe than a fighting axe, but it would serve my dad's purpose. He had his rifle, but that was more for group work than individual fighting. He waved me off the bike and told me to step back behind the vehicles.

"Get your bow ready, but don't take a shot unless you absolutely have to," Dad said.

"Why don't I just shoot him?" I asked, puzzled.

"Just listen to me. All right, he's seen us. Here he comes." Dad stepped away from the bikes and moved slowly along the road.

The Tripper growled and bared his teeth, his hands clenching into fists as he moved forward. His bloodshot eyes nearly glowed with anger, and his blotchy skin seemed to become even more inflamed. He was a normal man, dressed in a long sleeve shirt and jeans, but he was well beyond infected. His mouth was dark from biting, and his neck was scratched and had bled in the past. His hair was wild, sticking out above his ears, giving him a maniacal look. If Trey and I had found this guy, we might have wet our pants before we ran away.

Dad never stopped moving. He stood well away from me and held the axe low and to the side. I realized at that moment that I had never seen my dad kill anything without using bullets.

The Tripper sped up, reaching out with one hand while keeping the other near its chest. The outstretched arm threw its balance off a bit, and its torso swung around and back and forth. If I had to take a shot at that moment, it would have been luck to score a hit.

Suddenly, Dad sprang forward, running three steps towards the Tripper. He jumped up a little, and kicked the Tripper in the hip, knocking him sprawling. Dad didn't hesitate, stepped up quickly, and buried the head of the small axe into the top of the Tripper's head. The Tripper's arms and legs dropped to the ground and lay still. Dad yanked his axe out and plunged it several times into the dirt by the road. He then wiped it on the dead man's shirt, adding to the streaks already there. Dad pulled the man over to the ditch and tossed him in, removing him from the road.

I let out the breath I didn't realize I was holding and released the tension on the bowstring. I waited for my dad to come back over. The whole episode took about a minute, I think.

"Nice job," I said, as my dad stepped over his bike.

Dad looked at me. "Thanks. Tell me, Josh. What would you have done if it was you?"

I thought a minute. "Do I have the axe?" I asked.

"No, just what you have on *you*."

Hmm. A challenge. All right. "Since he's bigger, I would have probably parked the bike on the road and waited behind it and got my bow ready for when he fell." I said.

"Why would he fall?" Dad asked.

"Because he would try to walk through the bike and would trip over it."

"You'd kill him on the ground?"

"Just as dead as I could," I said, trying to sound tough.

Dad laughed out loud which told me my efforts were wasted. "Good enough, Josh. You'll do. You used your head before you used your strength. Nice."

CHAPTER 14

We rode in silence, and I felt very light headed for some reason. We rode until we reached a small house that stood on a decent sized hill. Dad said we would stop here for a drink and a bite to eat. Also to have a look around, he said, and this was the highest house around.

The driveway was tucked in the front yard with two concrete walls holding back the grass and dirt. The house stood on what looked like a plateau compared to the surrounding land. Dad said the rest of the land used to be higher, but when they put the road in, they cut lower and wound up putting the house up on a hill. I thought that was pretty silly.

I got off my bike and put down the kickstand. I waited for my dad, but he turned his bike around and leaned it against the far wall.

"How come you're putting your bike like that?" I asked.

Dad shrugged. "In case we have to get out in a hurry. I can grab and go while you're trying to get your bike turned around and the kickstand up. While they're killing you, I can make a good getaway."

I thought about that for half a second, then turned my bike around and leaned it against the same wall. I refused to look at my dad while I did it, but I could just *feel* his smile on the back of my head.

We approached the house slowly with my dad in front and me off to the side. I had my bow in my hand, but I didn't have an arrow nocked. Dad had his sidearm belted on, but he kept his hands away from it. Before we went to the house, my dad explained we would have to come up friendly since anyone who might be in the house would have the advantage and get one of us before we had a chance. Dad didn't think the house was occupied, but it never hurt to be ready.

The brush covered yard was quiet, but I saw out of the corner of my eye a rabbit or two slipping off to safer territory. Dad was about ten feet from the porch when he called out.

"Hello the house!"

Silence.

Dad tried one more time, then stepped up to the porch. The house had a wide porch that covered half the front and the entire west side. The tall windows on the house were still intact, and the upper windows had shutters on them that were closed. The porch had leaves and debris on it, but it looked okay.

The front door was closed, and my dad walked slowly to the windows and looked in, trying to see if anything was inside.

Finally, he shrugged and tried the door. It was locked but loose. Dad pulled out his pocketknife and worked the point into the space between the door and the jam.

"These old locks are pretty simple, Josh. The door is actually open; the only thing the lock does is keep the exterior handle from turning. All you have to do is move the latch out of the way. Use the point of your knife, and push it to the side." Dad pushed and levered something in the door. "Like so." He pushed the door, and it swung open without protest.

Huh. I'll have to remember that one. Handy. "Does it work with all locks?" I asked.

"No, just certain ones. Sometimes if you're in a hurry, it's easier to just smash the silly thing in," Dad said.

We stepped into the house and it was nicely furnished, although somewhat sparse. Dad called out again, but we didn't receive any reply. We walked through the house, and there was a fine layer of dust all over everything. No one had been here in years; maybe even before the Trippers arrived. I went upstairs and looked around. Two of the rooms were completely empty, and the third, the master bedroom, had a bed without covers, a dresser, and a small dresser near the bed.

I looked in the closet and didn't see anything, so I went over to the window to look out across the land. Flipping open the curtains, I coughed as the dust flew in my face

"Glad I did that," I said reproachfully to myself as my eyes watered. The open curtains showed me that I still had to open the shutters, and to do that I needed to open the window. I almost gave up but decided a look was worth it. Cracking the window open, I reached through and pushed on the shutters. Nothing happened. I looked it over and saw there was a latch on the shutters. That made sense. Opening the window further, I flipped the latch and pushed the shutters wide open.

Sunlight poured in through the window, and all the dust in the air sparkled like an indoor snowstorm. I waved my hand through some of the dust, swirling it around, and watching it hover in the air.

Outside, the landscape stretched before me. I could see for miles, and it was fascinating. I had never been this high above the ground before. I could see a highway and a small town off to the east, but not much further than that. I could see several other farmhouses in the distance, and some had big silver buildings that shone brightly.

I turned back, and as I did I looked into the closet again. Up in the corner of the shelf was a small box I hadn't seen before. I went over and had to reach up as high as I could, but I managed to grab it.

The box was redwood, and was secured with a simple lock on the front. I had no clue where to look for the key, so I just left it alone. The box had more dust on it than everything else, so I figured it had been there for a long time, before even the end times.

I took the box and went back downstairs where I found my dad waiting at the kitchen table. He had broken out some jerked beef, some water, and a few corn biscuits. There were dried apples, too, so we were eating well.

Dad's eyes found the box immediately. "What do have there?" he asked.

"Don't know. I found it in a closet upstairs." I handed it over to my dad, and he took it carefully from me.

"Heavy enough. We'll take a look in it later after lunch when we stop again." Dad brushed the dust off the box and found a place in his backpack for it. He resumed his lunch, and I ate mine. We didn't talk much, and that was okay with me. Sometimes I found it better to be quiet and let other people fill in the silence. I had learned that trick from my dad who usually used it on my mom. That was how he got her to talk instead of just letting her be quiet all the time. I used it on Trey, but he never really needed an excuse to talk.

We finished eating and started for the door. Just before I pulled it open, my dad suddenly grabbed me by my pack and pulled me back.

"Shh!" he said quietly as he stepped back slowly, carefully making no sound.

I looked around but didn't see any danger. I looked at my dad, but he was slowly pulling me back again, this time carefully to the stairs. We stood at the landing which kept us from being seen from the outside, but it also only gave us a view of the front door. We could see through the small window out towards the porch, but that was it.

"What is it?" I asked quietly, already knowing the answer.

CHAPTER 15

"Trippers." Dad said, pulling out his pistol. It was a small black gun that dad called his 'Glock', whatever he meant by that. I was familiar with guns through my readings and knew we were in some trouble if Dad got his weapon out. I put an arrow on my string and waited, trying to become part of the furniture.

Outside, I could hear the Trippers as they stomped up the steps to the porch, and they were noisy as they pounded up the wooden stairs. They moved around, but because we couldn't see them, they had no reason to rush the house since they couldn't see us either.

One Tripper reached the front door, and I could see the top of its head as it checked the door out. I held my breath as the handle jerked back and forth violently and then twisted as the Tripper tried to open it. Thankfully my dad had locked the door behind him as was his habit. Lessons from the bad times he always said.

The Tripper stayed by the door, then it's head slowly started to tilt back and raise higher as the infected person started to look in.

Suddenly there was a sparkle of glass falling to the floor. An arrow jutted out of the small window, stuck in the head of the Tripper. The infected person fell back, pulling the arrow through the small window. There was a huge thud as the Tripper slammed into the porch, and I felt the vibration as it shook the house.

My dad hissed at me. "Why did you do that, Josh?" he sounded angry as he listened for the other Trippers to react to the noise.

"Do what?" I asked. I was very confused. I looked down and saw my bow was in its usual place. My fingers felt like I had shot something, but for the life of me I had no recollection of doing anything like that.

"You just killed a Tripper right through that window!"

I thought about it for a second, and it came back to me. I knew we would be in danger if that Tripper saw us, and if my dad had taken a shot, then we would have really been in trouble. So I just automatically did what I had to do.

I explained it to my dad very quietly, and he calmed down when he realized I had done what was necessary, and to have delayed would have caused trouble.

"I'm sorry, Josh. I guess I didn't expect you to be on autopilot just yet," Dad said.

"That's okay," I said, putting another arrow on my bow. I wasn't entirely sure what 'autopilot' meant, but I made a note to ask later. Right now I had other worries. Another Tripper was thumping around to the front door and had a good chance of spotting us. I raised my bow, but my father pushed my arm down.

"The one you killed is in the way, so we might get lucky. Just hunker down, and we'll hope for the best," Dad said.

I sat on the bottom step trying not to breathe or move. I decided to treat this like a hunting situation. I needed the prey to move to a place where I could get a good shot, and I just needed patience.

My father wasn't doing as well. He fidgeted, he inspected his gun, he tied and re-tied his shoelaces. At one point I thought he might just stand up, go over to the windows, and start blasting away. I never knew he was so impatient. I began to wonder how he ever hunted before I was able to.

Finally, after what seemed to be an hour, the crowd stumbled off the porch and wandered away. My dad slowly went over to each window and carefully looked out.

"I think they're finally gone, Joshua. Let's get ourselves away from here in case they decide to come back," he said.

I couldn't agree more. I was tired of this house and wanted to get outside where it wasn't dusty. My throat was sore, and my eyes stung a bit.

We got back on our bikes and rode off to the east again, sticking to the shadows on the south side of the road. We carefully looked over each home we passed, but didn't see any more signs of trouble. Several of the homes were broken into, and more than a few had been burned. We just kept riding, and another hour found us on the outskirts of a town called Crete. I knew about Crete from my studies with my mom, so I thought it was odd that they would name a town after a Greek island.

Dad used his binoculars to look over the town, and what he saw must have been reassuring because he put them away and rode off without so much as a 'What do you think, Josh?'

I followed along, and my thoughts drifted here and there. I could see the town in front of me, and I wondered what it was like before the infection took over. Were there lots of kids like me? What were they doing; what did they do for fun? I couldn't imagine what it must have been like to just walk out of your house and not have to worry about someone trying to kill you because their mind was gone.

The town was pretty empty. We rode past a couple houses that looked like they had people living in them, and there was a man who was tending a garden who threw us a wave as we rode past. My dad rode over to talk, and I stayed put, content to just sit on the side of the road and watch the world slowly move on by. I amused myself by imagining places where Trippers might be hiding and figuring out ways to deal with them without getting killed.

After a bit Dad came riding back. He looked happy, like he was glad to have some kind of conversation other than with his son and his wife.

"Man says we're about ten miles from the wall; should be an easy run through the back country, and then we're there," Dad said.

"Will we get there before dark?" I asked. I was a little afraid we wouldn't have decent shelter and would have to camp out in the open. Trippers were especially active at night, and they could find you in the darkest of places. It was like they could hear your heartbeat or something.

My father understood my fear. "Don't worry, Josh. We'll find a safe place before it gets dark, don't worry."

We rode on and passed a huge grocery store and hardware store. We didn't bother to stop because places like that had been cleaned out a long time ago. You found stuff in homes, not in stores. Like the box I found in that farmhouse. We hadn't opened it up yet, but that was how you found things.

We caught a break and got to coast down a long, lazy hill that wound through a little valley of trees and a creek. I really liked the area, and said so to my Dad.

"This would be a nice place to live when I get my own house," I said, pointing to the trees and water."

"Someday you will Josh, but it's up to you to make it as safe as possible for your family," Dad said.

"I will," I said, and I meant it as a promise not to him, but to myself.

CHAPTER 16

We rode up a steep hill, and from the top I could see the grey wall. I had heard of it, saw a picture of it, but it was something else to see it in person.

We followed the road to where it abruptly ended and carefully approached the wall. The concrete structure simply cut the road off, no warning at all. The wall was about twenty feet tall and made of solid concrete. It was rough, but it had a strange beauty to it. I reached out and put a hand on it, looking up to the top as it towered over me.

My dad watched me for a while before he spoke. "Back when we had television, we were told this was going to happen. They said the only way to save the country was to protect the one place that was left; that had the fewest infected. They came in helicopters, Josh, carrying these pieces of wall. Bulldozers cleared the way while massive diggers cleared a trench to put the wall in. What was left of the army guarded us, and then they left to fight against the Trippers. Someplace east, if I remember. The city was included in the wall although there were a lot of infected people there. At the time, we thought the Trippers were just going to die out, but that didn't happen."

Dad put his hand on the wall. "We were told we were the last and had to fight. If we wanted a country and a future, it was up to us. After a couple of years, we realized we were the only ones left, and everything on the other side of this wall was either a Tripper or dead."

I didn't know what to say. Dad had never spoken to me about the real early years; mostly it was about how he had fought against looters and gangs, and how the sick were suddenly everywhere. But the original days, no. This was new to me.

My father continued. "We didn't know what to do. Some people left their homes and tried to go to the bigger communities, but that turned out to be a mistake since things were worse there with the Trippers all over. A lot of our neighbors left, and we've never seen them again. Trey's dad and I decided to make our stand at our homes, and we'd lend each other a hand as needed." Dad took his hand off the wall. "Turns out that was the only choice we could make. I had you and your mom to look after, and I have to say I really hoped everything would just move past us if we just left it alone."

I looked back at the wall. I could see how it would stop Trippers from coming over. I had a brief thought about how it stopped people from the other side trying to escape the madness of their world gone upside down.

"Have you ever looked over the wall, Dad?" I asked.

My dad shook his head. "Nope. As far as all of us were concerned, that world doesn't exist anymore." He picked up his bike and turned it around. "Besides," he said, "no one who's ever crossed that barrier has ever come back. No one." He emphasized that last point to make it clear to me that I should not have any thoughts about seeing what's on the other side.

We rode away as the sun was starting to set. The little valley with the trees and the creek was beckoning, and I was hopeful we would be able to spend the night in one of the homes. I was very happy, therefore, when my dad turned up a driveway and approached one of them. It was a small, single-story house made to look like a log cabin. I had seen pictures of log cabins, but this was a modern version. The yard was very overgrown, and the trees had dumped several years' worth of leaves on the roof. There was a garage around the corner of the house, but the roof on it had collapsed a while ago, largely in part to the huge tree branch sticking out of the center.

My dad parked his bike and cautiously approached the house. The air was eerily still in this part of the valley, and I could hear the creek happily bubbling along as it made its way eventually to the river. My hunter's eye saw several game trails, and I could see in my peripheral vision the furtive movements of small animals as they tried to see who the intruders were.

The sound of glass breaking brought me back to the task at hand, and I looked to see my dad reaching through a small side window by the front door and opening it. He went in carefully and about fifteen minutes later returned.

The sun was about an hour away from setting, and I noticed this valley was a lot darker than the surrounding land. I hoped we would be inside soon because Trippers liked the dark, and I could imagine several thinking this would be a nice place to spend a rage-filled nightmare of an existence.

"It's clear, Josh. Come on in. Put your bike up by mine." He indicated his parking space which was up by the porch but out of sight of the road. There wasn't any real danger of theft anymore. Most of the thieves had settled down or been killed. Dad told me once that the gangs tended to kill each other, and when the dust settled, the regular people then settled the gang. I never saw one myself, so I guess it worked.

We camped in the main living room, and while I took care of the gear, my father started a small fire in the fireplace. It was cool enough outside that I knew the night was going to be cold, and a fire would be welcome. The house was small but cozy, and besides the slight layer of dust, it was neat as could be. I imagined an older couple living here, or maybe a young man by himself. Heck, maybe I'd take it over when I got older.

Dad and I didn't talk much, but tonight he seemed to be in a mood to chat. "Josh, I don't know what the world will hold for you. I don't know what you will do for a living, if there is such a thing to be had anymore. I do know you're a skilled hunter, and based on how well you've taken to training, I think you'll do okay on your own.

"But I'm not always going to be here, and neither is your mom. So listen carefully because there are things it's time you learned."

Dad spoke on into the coming dark, and I never listened so carefully to what he had to say. It was as if he had been rehearsing this speech most of his life and was waiting for the right time to let it go. As I listened, I realized this was something I may want to do with my own children someday—give them a speech to guide and protect them. I drank it in like sweet rain, and it touched me deeply. More so than anything else I had ever been taught.

It was pitch black out when my dad finished. He reached over and messed my hair, then dug into his pack. He pulled out the box I had found and placed it on the floor between us.

"Well, let's see what you found here." Dad opened the box, and looked inside. He smiled to himself, and I heard him whisper "Perfect." He looked up at me, and the curiosity must have been on my face because he chuckled.

"Well done, Josh. Well done," Dad said, turning the box around.

I looked in, and my jaw dropped. I had seen pictures of them and read about them in my western novels, but I never thought I'd ever find one. Looking up at me, glinting in the firelight, was a nickel-plated Colt Single Action Army. It rested in a blue satin bed with bright white grips. In the bottom left of the box there was a small section that held five rows of bullets. I quickly counted them, and there were twenty-five in all. Each one was bright brass, and I could read the lettering on the back which said '45 Colt.'

My dad picked up the gun and opened the loading gate. I knew all about these from my books. He pulled the hammer to half-cock and gave the cylinder a spin. It clicked sweetly in the light, and my dad closed the gate. He uncocked the gun and put it back in the case.

"You'll have to learn to shoot now although I'm not sure you'll find too much 45 Colt ammo," Dad said.

"Me?" I squeaked. My heart was in my throat. Did he just mean what I thought he meant?"

Dad laughed. "Yes, you. You found it; it's yours. I have several, so I don't need another. Don't worry. I'll teach you how to use it, and more importantly, when to use it. Nice find, Josh."

Dad put the beautiful gun back into the case. He closed the lid, then slid the box over to me. I just looked at the box for a long time, then tucked it into my backpack. My mind was already spinning with what I was going to tell Trey, and I started thinking about what I could make a holster out of. These happy thoughts put me to sleep as the small fire in the fireplace cast red shadows all over the room.

CHAPTER 17

My dad woke me in what I considered a rude manner in the morning. His hand was over my mouth, and he waited until I had fully awakened before he took it away. When he did, he told me something that made me wish he had kept his hand on my mouth so I could yell appropriately.

"There's Trippers all around us. Stay on the floor, get your stuff, and very quietly get over to the door. Stay away from the windows," Dad said as he slowly crawled to his gear and started packing it up. It didn't look easy trying to do that while lying down, and when I tried it, I found it wasn't.

I got my stuff together and slowly made my way to the front door. Fortunately, there were curtains on the windows, so there wasn't a good chance of being seen. But by the front door there weren't any, so any Tripper looking in might have a chance of seeing us. I didn't understand my dad's logic, but here we were.

In a minute, my dad joined me. "You okay?" he asked. His gun was in his hand, and he was sweating slightly. I was sweating as well, since my bow was unstrung, and it was little more than a curvy stick right now.

"Okay. I'm going to go to the back door and start making some noise. When they clear out of the front, get to your bike and get riding, don't wait for me," he said.

"But, Dad!" I whispered in protest.

"No, Josh. I need you to get away, and I don't want to have to worry about you if I'm trying to get away, too."

"But..."

"Do what I say, Josh. I'll be fine. Be ready to move." My dad gave me a quick kiss on the top of my head and then slipped away to the back door. I couldn't see him, but in a second I could hear him.

"Hey! Hey! Right here! Right here!" he shouted.

I jumped slightly when I heard a couple of shots. I used the few seconds I had to string my bow and get it ready just in case. I wished I knew how to use my new gun, but I'd probably shoot myself in the leg.

I looked out the window and saw the front was clear of Trippers. I saw two of them stumbling around the side of the house, and I knew it was time to go.

"I'm out, Dad!" I yelled as I yanked open the door. Two more shots sounded, and I heard my dad yell out.

"Go, Josh! Move!"

I leapt down the stairs and sprinted towards my bike. I pulled it off the bush and rode like a lunatic towards the end of the driveway. I was at the road, about fifty yards away from the house, when I stopped. I know my dad told me not to, but I couldn't just leave. I saw movement. I saw my dad run through the house pursued by a very fast Tripper. Just as he got to the door and tried to close it, the Tripper grabbed his shirt. My dad was pulled around, and I could see the rage in the Tripper's face as its head darted forward to try and bite my dad's face off.

My dad's hand went up and punched the Tripper in the chin which gave him time to get his other hand up, the one with the gun, and shoot the infected man in the face. The Tripper went down without a sound, but the delay allowed two more Trippers to get close to my dad. One reached for his legs while the other grabbed his gun arm.

My dad let out a bellow of rage—a sound I had never heard before. It scared the hell out of me and finally got me moving.

"Dad!" I screamed, whipping an arrow out of my quiver. I nocked and fired so fast I had a second arrow ready to go before the first one hit the target. My aim was true; the Tripper at my dad's waist got an arrow through the top of her head, which killed her instantly. My second arrow stayed in my bow as my dad was in the way, and I didn't have a shot.

"Go, Josh! *Ride, dammit!*" my dad yelled. "*Go!*"

I was crying as I rode up the street, not knowing what to do. I stopped at the top of the hill watching the road behind me for any movement, anything. Tears streamed down my face as I cried in frustration. I wished I was bigger, I wished I knew how to shoot my gun, I wished all the Trippers would just die.

I sat down with my bow cradled in my arms, and I just rocked back and forth. I didn't know what else to do. I stared at the road until I had to blink, then stared at it some more.

CHAPTER 18

Suddenly, I saw something. I stood up to see better and there was my dad! He was pedaling furiously, and there was three Trippers chasing him, but with every turn of the pedal he got further and further away. I got on my bike and started to ride, and he caught up to me in short order. We rode for a little while, then stopped when it looked like weren't going to be pursued any further.

I jumped off my bike and ran over to my dad, throwing my arms around him. He hugged me back, and it was a minute before we spoke.

"You okay?" I asked, looking him over.

"Thanks to you," he said. "Your arrow gave me the seconds I needed. Thanks for not listening." My dad gave me another hug with his left arm, then let me go. "Come on, we need to put some miles on these bikes. I want to be home before lunch."

I could have pedaled all day; I was so happy to have my dad back. Everything seemed to be especially bright this morning for some reason, and I was glad for it. Nothing like a little run in with death to really clarify your vision.

We rode for a long time, passing by some of the same scenery we had seen on the way out. I was glad to have made this trip with my dad, but at the same time I had to wonder what the point really was. I'm glad my dad had a chance to talk to me, but we could have had a campout back in the yard.

We were about ten miles from home when we saw a small caravan heading south. It was about ten wagons long, and there were several horses and bikes. My dad waved to one of the men riding alongside, and the man rode over to greet us.

"Hello! You moving north?" the man said. He was a tall man, made taller in the saddle, and had the weathered look of so many people. His blue eyes were sharp, though, and I could see him taking in my father's badge, gun, and my bow. His eyes lingered on my dad, but he didn't say anything.

My father answered. "No, west. We're about ten miles from home. What's wrong?"

"Tripper wave, said to be bad, coming out of the city. Ask me, every one of those subdivisions should be burned to the ground." The man spat and looked north. "They'll be here in a day, maybe less. Two communities already went down. We're heading to the river."

My heart sank. I had seen two Tripper waves in my life, and it was always bad. For whatever reason, the infected sometimes decided to walk in a huge group, and they swept away everything in their path. The only thing you could do was hunker down and hope they passed by. If they found you, they'd tear your house down to get you. Our stone wall kept us safe both times, but it was a near thing.

"Thanks. I have to get home; my wife is waiting," Dad said.

"Good luck, then." The man turned his horse and rode away, leaving us at the road.

My dad shook his head. "We have to ride, Josh. We have no choice."

I shrugged. What else could I do? We couldn't stay out here, and if a wave hit our house, mom would probably lose it if we weren't there.

We rode as hard as we could without taking breaks, and the miles went past slowly. In the north we could see plumes of smoke rising in the air, and we knew the wave was coming. A half an hour later, we were throwing our bikes into the stable and securing them. Dad's horse bucked a bit, but she settled when we fed her.

Inside the house, my mom smiled when she saw us both, and then her smile turned to a frown as she looked at my dad.

"What happened?" she asked.

"Nothing. Got into it a little with some infected over by the wall. Nothing serious. Josh took one out; I took out another. No big deal." My dad tried to sound casual, but there was something in his voice that alarmed my mom and me.

"Let me see your arm," Mom said.

"I'm fine. Just a scratch from a branch. No worries, really."

"Show me."

My dad sighed and rolled up his sleeve on his right arm. On his wrist was a bloody mark, and it was easy to see the semi-circular pattern on the edge. The wound was red and angry looking, and my world turned upside down when I saw it.

A Tripper wave was coming, and my dad was infected.

CHAPTER 19

I didn't know what to say or do. I just looked at my dad and his injured arm. My mother put her hands up to her face and just started crying. I felt like doing just that, but I couldn't get past the feeling of being empty.

My dad broke the silence. "Look, I'll be okay for a while. We know it takes a while before the worst of it hits. I'll get everything as squared away here as I can. Once I'm gone, it's up to the two of you if you want to stay or go to a larger community. Right now, I'm going to clean this up and get ready for the Tripper wave. Josh, you need to help. Maria? I'll need some help with this wound."

My mom looked up at my dad like he was crazy, but she helped him anyway. She wrapped her arms around his waist and helped him upstairs. I noticed she kept her hands away from his injured arm. I would have, too.

I shook myself to get moving, and I went out to the garage. I tried to keep myself busy by getting the window covers, but my hands kept slipping and I kept dropping them on the floor. When I went to pick them up, I had a hard time because my hands were shaking so badly.

Finally, I rounded up as many as I could carry and took them inside the house. They were labeled on the inside, and I placed each one by its appropriate window. After I had gathered each one, I went around and put them over the windows themselves, latching them in place. The covers weren't anything more than plywood, but they were meant to keep the Trippers from seeing or hearing anything that would get them to attack. I had hoped we wouldn't need them anymore, but for some reason the damn Trippers kept coming back. I couldn't help but wonder if that's how we all were going to end up one day, just wandering around in a daze, slowly decaying away until we eventually die. I wish they all would die right now.

After I put the covers in place, I opened the small window my dad had cut in each one. It was a small square right in the center.

It was too small for a Tripper to fit through, but it was big enough to have plenty of angles to shoot them away.

I didn't do anything other than close the drapes on the upstairs windows, and I looked in on my dad. He was washing his arm and his wound, cleaning it out as well as he could. It was a nasty bite, but since it had gone through his shirt first, there was a hope he wasn't too deeply infected. I had heard some people had been bitten and managed to not turn, so if it wasn't a bad bite maybe my dad would be okay.

He caught me looking, and he glanced over at my mom who was sitting on the edge of the bed. She was lost in a daze, just looking out the window, not really doing much at all.

"Hey, Josh! Seems like it wasn't as deep as I thought. Maybe there's a chance after all. Help me with the bandage, would you?" My dad tried to sound cheerful and light, but I could hear the strain in his voice.

"Sure," I said. I went over to the sink and took the roll of bandages. Dad held the sterile pad over his cut while I wrapped it up a few times. I tied it off and then cut the extra.

"Good work," Dad said. "Let's check the defenses, shall we?"

"How does it feel, dad?" I asked, my curiosity overcoming my fear for a moment as we worked our way around the rooms and then headed downstairs.

"Actually, Josh, not that bad. Hurt at first, but now it just stings a little." He looked at me. "Wouldn't recommend you go and get your own, though."

I smiled, but I knew he was just trying to make me feel better. I didn't know what I felt. I was scared, worried, and uncertain all at the same time. What if my dad turned? Would I have to kill him? What would my mother do? What would I do? How could I keep up this house? Would we go to a community? I just didn't know.

We checked the downstairs preparations, and dad sent me out to collect some extra buckets of water and to make sure the horse was secured in her stall. I gave her an extra helping of hay, and she seemed to be content with the proceedings. I think I was a little jealous of her.

After that, there was little to do but sit around. We stayed upstairs because the house was very dark on the first floor. The window covers were very effective, and only a little light showed around the portholes. If I stayed down there I could see a little, but it wasn't easy. I went into my room and started making more arrows. I was nearly out of materials, but I did the best I could with what I had.

After I had made about two dozen, I pulled a couple of books off the shelf and dove in. They were westerns, naturally, since I was the proud new owner of a Colt. That thought sobered me a bit when I thought about what that Colt had cost me. Or might cost me; we'll see.

CHAPTER 20

The sun was slipping past the horizon when I looked out the window. That was when I saw the first one. She was young, about my age, and was moving slowly through the trees. Her blonde head swayed a little from side to side, and her arms were out in front a bit to give her a little balance. She was wearing a sweater and some jeans, and I could make out some dark marks on her face. As she got closer, I saw those marks were blood stains. She looked around, scanning for threats, and moved along our western wall. She was about fifty feet from where I was, and I could have easily killed her with an arrow, but I didn't dare make a sound. Her angry cries would draw everyone around for a mile, and I had enough to worry about.

I watched her stumble past, and happened to look over at my neighbor's house. It had been empty for years, and there was nothing of any use in there. The only thing it was good for was firewood. Dad and I had torn up the oak floorboards from the two bedrooms last winter when the snows were really bad.

After her came two more—young men by the looks of them. One had a knife sticking out of his shoulder, and the other was dragging a broken foot. I remembered the arrow I had put in the chest of another Tripper, and I couldn't help but wonder why that one died but this one seems to be doing just fine.

Suddenly, the two stiffened and they stared at the house next door. I looked up and saw that someone was there! There was a person standing in the downstairs window, and with the last sunlight drifting through the building, they were outlined as clear as day. The Trippers began to move up to the house, and whoever was there wasn't very bright, because they moved quickly to close the curtains.

That was it. The Trippers howled and rushed the house, one reaching it sooner than the other with the broken foot, but they started to pound on the window they saw the person in. The noise brought back the blonde from before, and there were six more that came over the yard and advanced on the house.

"Dad!" I whispered, walking away from the window. "Dad!" I went into my parent's room, and found my dad reading a book.

"What is it Josh?" He looked up from his reading. I caught the cover and it said 'Triggernometry', whatever that might be.

"Trippers are at the house next door," I said quietly, even though I wanted to shout it.

My mother looked up from her work, glanced at my dad and said, "So it begins."

"There's no one there, so no worries Josh. They can't get over the wall," he said.

"But there is someone there! They were in the window, and the Trippers saw them!"

Dad put the book down and followed me as I ran back to my room. I could hear the banging as the Trippers pounded on the windows and walls of the house next door.

Dad looked out. "Jesus," he said.

And how. I looked out and saw nearly fifty of the infected creatures. They came in all shapes and sizes, and every one was trying to get into the house. If anyone was in there, I hoped they had put themselves into the attic and were being quiet in a corner.

A crashing of glass, a screech of triumph, and the infected were in. They streamed through the broken window and flooded the house. We watched them as they roamed around the downstairs and figured it was only a matter of time before we saw them upstairs.

A few minutes later, we were right. And a second after that we heard a scream. It was a deep, painful scream, like someone who had just lost a best friend or loved one. Suddenly it was cut off, and there was a frenzy of activity in one of the rooms. I was grateful I couldn't see into the room.

Outside, the Trippers who hadn't gone in were milling about. But they got excited when a boy about my age came tearing out of the broken window. His arms were torn and bitten, and it looked like he had been given a bloody nose. But he was moving, and might have made it if he hadn't run full tilt into another group of Trippers.

He yelled as they pounded and tore at him, biting and clawing his flesh away. When he fell to the ground, they fell with him, beating and tearing. His yells turned to screams as they ripped his abdomen open, and ropes of intestines were thrown into the air. He stopped screaming when they tore his heart out.

I could do nothing but watch. He was already infected, and would have been lost anyway. Being a Tripper was almost the same as being dead. It just took longer for the process to get done.

My dad looked at me and turned away, saying nothing. We were both probably thinking the same thing. What was going to happen to him? What was going to happen to mom and me? I wished I knew.

CHAPTER 21

During the night, the Trippers were all over the place. They never got inside the walls of our yard, and I could see that Trey's family was in as decent of shape as we were. The hard part was being quiet all the time and staying away from the windows.

In the morning, I amused myself by counting the Trippers first and then giving them names. There was Suzy, Frank, and Bill over by the shed, and there was Wendy, Maria, and Gordon hanging out by the old mailbox. There was Brandon by the big tree, and Holly headed over to the creek. There was Jessica along the wall, and inside the yard was my dad.

I shook my head and looked again. Sure enough, my father was crawling towards the wall with a small rifle in his hands and a box. I recognized the box and the rifle. The rifle was a .22 my dad had found a year ago. It was supposed to be a copy of a more powerful rifle, but it was still fun to shoot. It had a thingy on it that was supposed to make the gun shoot quietly, but it was just for show, as my dad said. But he tinkered with it and found that if he took the fake silent thing off and cut the barrel down, he could attach a big oil filter from a truck. When he fired it like that, it made almost no sound at all. Trouble was, we couldn't aim it very well. Why my dad had it now was very curious.

He made it to the wall, and I could see his bright white bandage nearly glowing in the early dawn. He looked up at me and gave me a small wave, then moved over to the wall. He stood up and rested the big filter barrel in a notch of the rocks. His head was clearly visible to the Trippers, but they hadn't seen him yet. I was nervous as hell, and went so far as to get my bow strung and stand by my window, ready to let fly.

But Dad seemed to know what he was doing. He made a sound, and the three nearest Trippers moved over to the wall. They made their way to him, and as the first one stuck his face in the notch, my dad shot him between the eyes. The Tripper's head snapped back, and he fell backwards like a tree. The next one strolled up, stuck his head in, and got nailed for it as well. I couldn't hear anything from where I was, and by the looks of the inactivity out there, the Trippers were unaware as well.

Dad managed to kill ten by the fence, and that was the end of the Trippers on that side. He crawled along the wall, then popped his head up to look around, ducking it back down before anyone saw him. He went over to where he saw the nearest Trippers and stuck his rifle over the top. I saw him looking through a hole in the wall, and then he did something to get the Tripper's attention. Several wandered over, and when they were lined up with his gun, he took them out. Another five added to the score. I was happy he was killing them until I realized I was going to have to help him clean up.

It went on like this for about an hour. Dad snuck around and killed Trippers as they came to investigate. As long as he kept himself out of sight, they wouldn't see him as a threat. I wondered if he had wrapped his head in tree branches, could he just walk around and shoot them? Something to think about.

When he finished, he snuck his way back in, and I could hear him fussing about downstairs. In a few minutes, he came into my room.

"What do you think?" he asked, looking out the window.

"I'd say you're about a hundred short, but a good start," I said. "How's the arm?"

Dad looked at his bandage. "Seems okay, a little tight, but that's about it."

We didn't say anything for a bit. We both knew that was the infection starting, and whether it was the virus or just his body reacting to the bite, we would know in a few days.

During the next couple of days my dad brought out the case, and we went over my new Colt. I practiced loading and unloading it, and I dry-fired it a few times. My dad taught me how to hold it with both hands, one hand, and how to aim without using the sights. I didn't get the chance to actually fire it, but it was for the better. If the Trippers got over our wall it would have been the end.

Trey and I communicated with each other off and on during the wave. We tied notes to our arrows and launched them towards each other's homes. I had to kneel on the ground and use a slanted hold on the bow, but I managed it all right. Trey had it easy. With a crossbow, all he had to do was lift it and shoot.

Trey was sad to hear about my dad and jealous about my Colt. But he said he and his family were doing fine. He saw the activity next door, and was sad someone had to die. His dad killed some Trippers like my dad had done, so at least we were accounting for a good number of them.

Two days later the Trippers wandered off. It wouldn't be safe to be very far from home for at least another week, so we were going to have to be really careful.

CHAPTER 22

My dad wasn't doing well. He stayed in bed, and at times had a bad fever. We knew he wasn't going to make it, and I was worried all the time about what I was going to do about him. I went up to see him, and it was shocking to see how much he had changed in just a few days.

"Hey, Josh," Dad said. He was covered in sweat, and his arm was swollen around the bite mark. His eyes were red and glazed and he was breathing heavily. "I'm glad I can remember your name," he said. "I can feel my mind slipping away. It's like I'm losing my memories one at a time." He took a small drink of water from the canteen by the bed. "I can't remember anything from my childhood. I tried, but I can't." He closed his eyes. "It's all going away. Nothing to be done for it."

I looked down not wanting him to see me cry. It was a few minutes before I could look up again. "Does it hurt?" I asked, worried about the pain.

"No, it doesn't. I don't feel any pain at all. I would get up, but I can't seem to remember how. It's all just flowing away. It's like my mind has a hole in it, and all the thoughts are leaking out," he said.

I hesitated, not wanting to ask the next question. "What do you want me to do, Dad?" I didn't want to hear the answer, but I knew I had to.

Dad sighed. A long, deep, soul-wrenching sigh. It was a moment before he answered. "I don't want to be one of them, Josh. They've turned me, but I don't want to be one of them."

I knew that was the answer, but it didn't make it any easier. I didn't say anything, I just let my tears fall on the floor. They hit with a wet smacking sound that seemed loud in the room.

"Your mom isn't doing well, Josh. You'll need to look after her when I'm gone," he said. "I think she might be going over the end." A spasm hit and he gasped, bringing his hand up to his head.

I watched through my tears, and I just slowly shook my head. "What can I do, Dad?"

My father slowly breathed in and out, and it was a while before he spoke. When he did, it was measured and deliberate. "I'm sorry, son, but I need you to be a man and to do what needs to be done. There's no one else."

In a way, I knew he was going to say that, but the spoken words just shook me worse than before. I didn't want to let him down, but I didn't want to have to kill him, either. And I really didn't want to let him turn into something that would try and kill me. Part of me wondered if it would be easier to kill him when he was fully gone, but I shook that thought out of my head. My dad didn't want to turn; he was clear on that.

"Better do it soon, son. I can feel it moving through my head. Remember I love you, and remember what I told you before. Like your books say, you'll do to ride the river with." Dad sighed again and closed his eyes.

I knew for certain that he wasn't going to open them again as my father.

I went downstairs and told my mother. She nodded, then looked out the window. She hadn't spoken much in the last week of the Tripper wave, and I couldn't blame her. Everywhere she looked she saw her husband. I told her it might be a good idea for her to go check on the horse for a bit or to go into the garden.

She looked sharply at me, and I held her gaze. She slowly nodded and moved to the back door. Once she was there, she looked back. "Thank you, Josh. I'm sorry for what you have to do. And I'm sorry for what may happen next." She left before I could ask what she meant, but I was distracted in a minute by a deep moan that came from upstairs.

I ran up the steps and turned to my room. I pulled out my Colt and loaded it with five live rounds. Snapping the loading gate shut, I made sure a round was ready to go, then went down the hall towards my parents' room.

Every step felt like I was moving through sand, and my gut was a twisted mess. The Colt felt like it weighed a thousand pounds as it slowly swung in my hand.

When I reached the door I looked in, and I knew I had to act. My dad's face was starting to get the splotches common to Trippers, and he was breathing quickly. In another few hours, he was going to get up on his own and go looking for people to kill.

I walked over to him and had a moment's hesitation as to where I should put the gun. I realized I couldn't shoot him in the head. As much as I knew it would kill him instantly, I couldn't do it. I decided on the next best thing. I knelt on the bed, next to my father, and placed the muzzle of the Colt over his heart. I pulled the hammer back, and the four clicks were the loudest things I had ever heard.

"Good bye, Dad. I love you," I said. I closed my eyes and pulled the trigger.

My father jerked from the impact, and I nearly dropped the gun. But I cocked the hammer back and waited to see if I needed to do it again.

As it turned out, my father was dead. His face was relaxed, and he looked more at peace than I had seen him in several days. I slid off the bed, uncocked the gun, then went to the bathroom to throw up.

I knew the job wasn't finished, because I couldn't just leave him there in the bed to rot. After I cleaned myself up, I went back into the bedroom and flipped the quilt he was lying on over his body. I flipped the other side over him and grabbed the blanket up by his shoulders. I pulled, heaved, and cursed as I levered his body off the bed. My dad fell with a huge thump that shook the house, and it was then I realized just how heavy the man really was. The craziest thought I had just then was how dangerous a Tripper he would have made.

I pulled him away from the bed, dragging him across the floor. I took a glance at the bed, expecting to see a hole and a lot of blood. I was surprised to see nothing. I guess the bullet didn't make it out of his body.

I got my dad's corpse out of the house, and the only trouble I had was when he got away from me on the stairs and thumped down to the landing. Other than that, it was just a heavy drag out into the side yard. By the time I reached the bed of hostas, I was exhausted. But I still had work to do, so after I took a quick drink, I got the shovel out of the garage and started digging.

It was late afternoon by the time I had finished. The grave wasn't all that deep, but it would have to do. I didn't think Dad would mind much; he probably would have appreciated the effort. I rolled his body into the grave, never bothering to take another look at him. I didn't want to have any more memories of his death than I already had, and I felt in some way it was my fault. If I had gone when he said to, if I hadn't been so far away when the Trippers attacked that house, I might have been able to buy him some time—something.

I cried again as I filled the grave, mounding the dirt slightly, and putting the hostas back where I had dug them up. They would look after him like they did everything.

I turned to put the shovel away and bumped into my mother.

"Jeez, mom! You scared me. How long have you been there?" I asked.

Mom just stared past me at the grave. She was holding a small handful of flowers, and without a word, she walked past and knelt down next to the grave. I wanted to comfort her, but I didn't know what to say. Nothing my dad ever taught me prepared me for this.

I put the shovel away, and I walked back to the house. I couldn't shake the feeling I was going to have to do more grave digging—and soon.

CHAPTER 23

Of all the chores I had, without a doubt the one I hated the most was removing bodies. It was slow, heavy, and smelly. I couldn't do it on my own; I just wasn't strong enough. But I wondered if any twelve-year-old would have been strong enough.

Fortunately, Trey was willing to help me if I was willing to help him. He was smaller than I was and even less likely to be able to move some of the bodies, so we had to work together. Especially since the last wave gave us about an even hundred bodies to get rid of.

Trey's dad was setting up the burn pile, so he was unable to give us a hand. My mother had withdrawn into herself for the last two days after my father died, so she was out of it. Trey had a younger sister, but she would have been a nuisance under the best circumstances, so here we were. Trey's older siblings were helping his dad.

"You got it?" Trey asked, readying the wagon.

"I got it. Get that thing over here; this one looks like it's leaking," I said, holding the arms of a dead woman. Her eyes had rolled up in her head, giving her a nasty appearance. The small round hole in her forehead didn't improve her looks.

"Ew."

"Exactly."

I pulled the body forward, doubling it over its waist. Trey tipped the wagon so the leading edge was on the ground. We both then took an arm and tipped the wagon back, ending up with a Tripper neatly riding a four wheeled cart. We then pulled it down to where Trey's dad was building a pyre.

It was a squat affair with several large logs forming a kind of hut. Trey's dad was finished with the base and was putting dead Trippers all over the logs.

"Drop the next bunch on the other side, boys; this side's full," he said, pulling up an older Tripper and placing him on the pile. Trey's dad would pile the bodies up around the structure, then put more logs on top, then more bodies. Hopefully he wouldn't have to go higher than two levels, but once we had to go as high as four. The logs were soaked with kerosene, and once lit, the blaze was going to be fierce. But it had to be done, and since we didn't use kerosene for anything other than lamps, we had enough to spare.

Towards the end of the day, we finally managed to get the last of the Trippers up onto the pyre. Trey's dad had set up a system where he could ignite the pyre from a distance. It wasn't anything fancy, just Trey's crossbow firing a flaming arrow into the heart of the structure. After that it was just a lot of burn time.

Evening came, and Trey and his father went back to their home for supper. We weren't going to light it at night unless we wanted to attract every Tripper for miles. The wave had moved on, but that didn't mean we were fully safe from them coming back.

I met my mother in the kitchen, which surprised me. She had holed herself up in the spare bedroom upstairs, and the last time I saw her she was just looking out the window at my father's grave.

"Hey, Mom!" I said, trying to sound somewhat cheerful. It was strained, and we both knew it. The gloom of my father's death hung over us like something unsaid.

"Hey, Josh. Looks like you've been working hard. Wash up, and we'll have supper," she said.

"Sure. Be right back." I went to the back room and quickly washed my hands, noting the level of water and making a note to head to the creek tomorrow for more.

At supper, we didn't have much to say, and I saw how thin and frail my mom looked. If we had another wave of Trippers come through, I wasn't sure how she would make it.

I had just finished eating when my mother spoke.

"Josh? I wanted to talk to you about something," she said, clearing the table.

"What about?"

"I think we should leave the house."

I was surprised, but at the same time, not really. I had been expecting something like this.

"Why? Where would we go?" I asked.

"One of the larger communities where its safe. This isn't safe anymore," she said.

"What's not safe? We have the wall; we have the water. The last wave didn't get us, and neither did the one before that," I said. I didn't want to go. I didn't want to leave my home and everything I knew.

"What about next time, Josh? And the time after that? Your father died…"

I didn't let her finish. "Dad died away from here. If we had stayed here, we'd have been fine."

"That's true, sweetheart, but he's gone, and we can't get him back." Mom looked down, and when she looked back up there were tears in her eyes. "Please, Josh. I don't want to lose you, too. Let's get out of here and go where there's other people; where you have a chance at a future and not just survival."

I gave it a thought. "Not right now, mom. I can't go right now. I don't think Dad would have wanted me to just up and leave."

Mom shook her head. "He wouldn't have wanted you to hold on to something that wasn't there, either."

I had nothing to say to that, so I just left the table and went upstairs with my mom calling after me.

CHAPTER 24

The next morning I went over to Trey's house, and together we headed out to our trap lines. It had been a long time since we'd been out that way, so chances were anything we had caught was inedible. But we would have to clear them out, so off we went.

As we reached the woods, I told Trey about my mother and what she wanted to do.

"Community?" Trey said. "Man, that's crazy. You ever been to one of those places?"

I shook my head. I had seen them, but never went to one.

"Dad took me over to the one out west. Can't remember the name, ended with a 'fort' or something. Anyway, it was all rules and regulations, and sharing everything, and people walking around just scared of their own shadow." Trey spat in disgust. "They made us check our weapons at the gate, and they meant everything. My little skinning knife, you know the one with the red handle?"

I only nodded, stunned at what I was hearing.

"Well, they took that and never gave it back. When my dad demanded it back when we were leaving, the men at the gate laughed in his face. Couldn't do nothing about it on account of them having heavy rifles." Trey looked at me. "They didn't keep it because they needed it. They kept it because they knew they could. When I look back on it, I think we were lucky to have left at all."

Well, this wasn't what I wanted to hear to help me change my mind about leaving. As a matter of fact, it made sure I wasn't going anywhere. I couldn't imagine having the knife my father gave me taken away.

The day seemed especially bright as we made our way up the hill towards our lines. The grass was much lighter green than it had been, a signal that the days were going to start getting colder. I was going to have to lay in a supply of firewood before too long, something my dad used to do. There were a lot of things I was going to have to take up now that I was the one to take care of the house. But my first priority was to make sure we could eat, so I was out here.

The trees were quiet this morning, only making noise with their top branches. The wind tried to stir things up a bit more, but the trees weren't having any of it. These were the old guard, the ones who were old long before we got here. My dad told me that they were likely around when the first colonists decided to rule themselves, and they were here for the big war between the states. There was respectable space between them, and I often wondered what they whispered to each other in the night.

A quick walk through the woods got us to our trap lines, and every single one was full. And every single catch was inedible. That was what I was expecting, and I hoped the carcasses didn't scare away the game to other trails. Trey and I worked our lines for the better part of an hour, and we reset them with new grass. I had to repair a couple, but other than that I figured it could have been a lot worse.

On our way back, Trey and I talked about the wave. "What did you do with yourself?" I asked, using the knife my dad gave me to slice off the tops of weeds.

"Played cards a lot, read some books, shot arrows at some fool who kept shooting them back," Trey answered. "Same stuff as last time."

I laughed. "Sounds like my house, only I was more productive since I made arrows."

"I don't miss as much as you, so I didn't bother," Trey said.

I laughed again, then got sober. "I killed my dad."

Trey looked at me, and his big brown eyes were sincere. "Sorry about it, man. I know it was rough. My dad said in his eyes you were a full-growed man to do that."

I liked that a lot, knowing Trey's dad, who I liked a great deal, was willing to count me as an equal. It didn't make me feel much better, but at least it didn't make it any worse.

On our way down we decided to make a small side trip. Neither of us had been out and about for the last several days, so we weren't willing to just stroll back and go inside. Trey and I decided to pay a visit to The Simpson's to see how they made out during the wave. We followed the road up around the hill and walked along the edge of the forest. The brush was impassable along this stretch with huge thorn bushes dominating the edge. Several had reached out across the road, and we were careful not to get scratched. With all the Trippers that were walking around here, the last thing I needed was to get sick because of some stupid shrub.

At the entrance to the subdivision we turned in, and immediately I wished we had gone home. Two Trippers were under the pine trees there and started crawling out when they saw us.

"Damn, man, what are we going to do?" Trey asked, hopping from one foot to the other.

I looked at the Trippers, and all I could feel was anger. I was mad at them for being what they are. I was mad because they were here, and my dad wasn't. I don't know what I was thinking, I just acted. I ran over to the nearest Tripper who was still on his hands and knees. He was a young one, maybe a few years older than I was, and he was thin, very thin in his stained t-shirt and jeans. I kicked him in the side of his head, knocking him to the dirt. I kneeled on his back, keeping him on the ground, and stabbed him in the back of the neck with my knife. The point slid in with nearly no resistance, and the Tripper ceased moving immediately.

The other infected man, a larger person wearing what looked like a formal suit, charged from the right, growling with rage. I waited until he was nearly on top of me, and then I dove out of the way, letting him trip on the body on the ground. He fell forward, cracking his head on the big limestone rock that once was used as a sign. He slumped to the ground, leaving a bloody trail down the rock. I waited for a minute, then figured he had managed to kill himself. I shoved the blade into the ground, then wiped it off on a relatively clean part of the Tripper's pants.

I stood up to find Trey staring at me. His mouth was open, and his knife hung loosely in his hand.

"What?" I was a little put off by his face which seemed to be a mixture of shock and awe.

"Dude, where the…I mean, damn! How the…okay, that was pretty cool. God, are you nuts?" Trey managed to get out.

"What? My dad and I trained for a while; he taught me a few things."

"Where the hell was I?" Trey asked. "How come you didn't invite me?"

"You were on punishment, remember?"

Trey's cheeks flamed. "Right. Remember that."

We walked around the road, keeping out of the deep grass that grew on the side of the road. We didn't have our bows with us, although I would have taken my Colt had I finished the holster I was making for it. I was copying a picture from a Western book, and it was taking time for the leather to cure and harden. I knew how to tan hides, having learned from my dad, but that made the skins soft, and I wanted the holster to be stiffer. I had told Trey about the gun already, but I was wanting to show it later. I knew he'd go nuts, and I wanted to enjoy that as much as possible.

As we walked, Trey and I talked about the weapons we possessed. I had my knife, and he had his, and we each had our bows, but we really didn't have anything that would work in a close fight.

"We need something that would kill them out of arm's reach from us," Trey said. "Something that would be quick, and I'm not talking about our bows," he added quickly as I opened my mouth.

"Not sure what would work," I said, stepping around a large stone. There was a long branch in the way, and I picked it up. For no other reason than the fact I was holding it, I threw it across the yard in an attempt to hit a small hanging sign by the house.

"Me either," Trey said. We stepped past the small brick ranch house on the corner, and neither of us tried to look to hard at the small pile of bodies huddled around the front door. There didn't seem to be any wounds on the people, so it wasn't easy to see if they were Trippers or squatters. Either way, it was creepy.

The road turned slightly, curving between two large trees, and we saw the Simpson's house. Right away we knew something was wrong. There were about a dozen dead Trippers in the yard, their blotchy faces marking them as clear as day. Nearly all of them had a crossbow bolt in their heads. That would have been the work of Lucy's brother. He was pretty good with his bow and was able to reload much faster than Trey ever could.

Trey and I shared a look, and we approached the house very carefully. The front door had been broken and was hanging off of one hinge. I stepped very carefully around a dead Tripper, trying to be as silent as possible.

Once both of us were in, I picked up a long pole that was one the ground. It was about four feet long and looked like it might have been the bar from a closet. Either way, it was a little comforting to have something other than my knife.

The kitchen was a disaster, with cabinets open and items thrown all over the place. The sink was piled high with old food and trash and covered with ants. Trey and I looked at each other again.

"You ever been in here before?" Trey whispered.

"No." I replied. "You?"

"Nope. Kind of messy."

"Yeah."

We moved towards the center hallway, and there was a body on the floor. It was a woman, and her face was pressed into the corner. Her right hand was up against the wall, and there was blood all over the place. Her back had been torn apart, and her neck was one shredded wound. It looked like someone had just torn chunks out with their teeth. Her legs were at weird angles, and one of her calves showed bite marks, too. She must have been bitten in the leg and fell here when she tried to get away. They sure finished her here.

"Josh, that's Lucy's mother," Trey said quietly.

"Damn," I said. I didn't say it, but I was pretty sure Lucy was not alive in here.

We stepped further back and looked into one of the bedrooms. Lucy's brother was lying on the bed, and it was pretty obvious how he died. He must have retreated here and tried to hold them off by shooting them with arrows, but he couldn't reload in time. The Trippers got hold of him and his remaining arrows and used them to kill him with. He had four arrows sticking out of his head and about ten more coming out of his body. I had never seen Trippers use a weapon before, so I was kind of fascinated with what they had done. But there was nothing left here, so we moved on to the next room.

The last room on the house was Lucy's, and we found her there. She was curled up in a little ball in the corner, and by the amount of blood around her body, she must have died relatively quick. Her back looked caved in on one side, and Trey took a closer look.

"They just kept hitting her. They crushed her ribs and just kept going. Chances are they beat her until they reached her heart. They just kept hitting her." Treys voice shook as he stepped away from Lucy.

I just shook my head. Another life gone. Another life wasted to these useless animals. I felt so helpless. There was nothing I could have done even had I been here to help. They just don't stop unless you put them down the first time.

"Come on, let's get out of here. This place is full of infection. If we don't wash, we're gonna turn," I said, stepping out the bedroom door and getting out of the house. I tried to sound tough, but I just wanted to leave. There was nothing here. It was such a waste. They had survived twelve years, lived through a bunch of waves, outlasted the looters and would-be warlords, and went down like this. It made as much sense to me as my father's death.

We walked out of the house, and Trey closed the door. It didn't matter if he left it open or not. Eventually it would fall to the elements or some wandering people would take what they could use. It was the way things were now.

CHAPTER 25

Trey and I didn't talk much as we walked back to our houses. We just kept our thoughts to ourselves. When we got to my fence, we split, and Trey looked back at me one last time. "Think I have an idea for a weapon. I'll work on it and let you know."

I shrugged. "Take your time. I'm going to head out to the trap lines day after tomorrow and start things over again."

"See you."

"See you."

I went into my house and hollered to my mom I was home. She came out of the back room and wiped her hand over her forehead.

"Hi, Josh. How's your lines?" she said.

I was a little taken aback. Mom never asked about the lines. "About what I had expected. We had to clear the carcasses and reset the lines, and with any luck they'll start producing again like before."

"How did Trey's family handle the wave?"

I shrugged. "'Bout the same. They're all okay over there."

Mom looked at me funny. "What's wrong, Joshua? You look upset."

I looked down. I tried to hide the tears coming down my face, but I couldn't. When I spoke I barely made a sound.

"The Simpsons are dead, Mom."

My mother came over and put her arms around me. I threw my arms around her and cried for what might have been a long time. I cried for Lucy, I cried for her family, and I cried for my dad. I just couldn't help myself. It just came in waves. "They beat them to death; just hit them till they died," I said.

Mom never said a word, she just held on to me, rocking slightly from side to side, and whispering 'It's all right Josh. It's not your fault. It's not your fault."

She held me for a long time, and when I finally cried myself out, she sent me up to my room to rest. She promised we would talk later, but for right now, I needed to sort it out for myself.

I went upstairs and lay down for a while. I must have fallen asleep, because when I opened my eyes again it was close to late evening. I went back downstairs and looked for my mom, but she wasn't in the house. I scanned the outside from the second floor, since I hadn't taken down the window covers yet. It was good practice to leave them up for a while, since Tripper waves never seemed to be limited to just one.

I didn't see my mother, and it was becoming a worry. She was never one for venturing too far away from the house, and she certainly wouldn't be wandering around the woods. I went back downstairs and went out to the small stable to look in on the horse. I let her out of the stall, and let her wander about the yard a bit. I was going to have to figure out what I was going to do with her since I wasn't a very good rider, and she was another mouth to feed. I would probably give her to Trey's family or just let her go. Eventually she'd find other horses and become someone else's ride.

I went back into the house and worked on my holster. It was going to be a cross draw job; pretty simple, but effective. I had read all about the gunfighters in my books, and while I would love to have a rig like theirs, low on the hip and ready to go, my world was a little more realistic. I needed to be able to sit and ride my horse and the cross draw made more sense.

Right before it got dark and we would be in for the night, I heard the back door open. I took my Colt with me and slipped down the stairs careful to make as little noise as possible. I didn't have to worry; it was my mom. She was taking off her shoes when I spoke.

"Hey, Mom. Where'd you go?" I slipped the Colt into my belt behind my back, keeping it out of sight.

"Oh! Josh! You scared me. Goodness." She ran a hand over her face, and waved the other one dismissively. "I was over to see Trey's mom. She and I hadn't talked in a while."

"Oh, okay. I walked the horse a bit. I'm thinking of letting her go," I said, wondering what Mom's reaction was going to be. I shouldn't have worried.

"Sounds good, Josh. Your dad would have wanted you to do that if you weren't going to keep her," Mom said.

I nodded. "All right, well, I'm going up to bed. It's dark and I'm tired for some reason."

"You've had a tough few days," My mother said. "Things will look better tomorrow."

I wanted to believe her, but something wasn't right about this whole situation. My gut told me something was wrong. But I had nothing but a feeling to go on.

CHAPTER 26

In the morning, I woke up, and the sun was decently high in the sky. I felt much better, having slept for so long, and the sunlight was a welcome change from the gloom that had been over us for days. I felt like today was going to be a good day, and I felt like that all the way until I looked out the window.

We were completely surrounded by Trippers, and there was enough to cover the distance between our house and Trey's.

I looked down at the sea of infected humanity and summed it all up in one word.

"Crap."

I had some serious concerns. There were enough of them to start climbing over each other and getting a leg up on our wall. That would be bad enough. Secondly, this many Trippers meant something seriously bad had happened up north, and this wave was more than just a random event. One of the communities must have had an outbreak, and they couldn't contain it. We were going to have to be extremely careful and hope they pass on soon.

I was worried about the horse. She was going to need to be fed and watered, and she was a long way away from the house. I wish I had put her in her stall in the garage, but that couldn't happen now.

Thinking about that horse gave me an idea. It was dangerous, stupid, and crazy, but I liked it immensely. If it worked, I wouldn't have to clean up bodies, and we wouldn't have to hide away much longer than a day. If it didn't work, I'd likely die a hideous death at the hands of the Trippers.

My mother would never go for it, so I'd have to work this one out on my own. I started packing a backpack and made sure I had everything I would need. I was going to have to leave the bow behind since there wasn't any way to ride a horse and hold on to it at the same time. Believe me, I've tried.

I slid the holster onto my belt and tried out the Colt. The heavy six-gun pulled my belt down in the front and threatened to pull my pants down. I tried walking with it, but it banged around my leg and hip, feeling extremely awkward. I pulled the gun out and took the holster off. Guess I was going to be taking my bow after all. The Colt wasn't going to be on my hip for a while, I guessed.

I went downstairs and saw my mom was already up. She smiled and asked me if I wanted any breakfast.

"No thanks. Did you see the Trippers?" I said, trying to sound casual.

"Yes, Josh. Thank you. I'll be careful down here," Mom said.

I tried to figure out what was going on. My mother was never this calm around a sea of Trippers. I had a bad feeling, but I couldn't pin down what it was about. As long as we were careful we were safe. Considering what I was about to do, though, I had no room to talk.

"I'm going to be checking on the horse, Mom, so be careful," I said, stepping towards the back door.

"I will. You too," she replied. She was humming to herself, seemingly completely at ease, and completely freaking me out.

I slipped out the back door as quietly as I could. This involved opening the door, crawling out, and closing it again. I moved carefully around the house, staying to the shadows, and getting into the garage. I needed my stuff from there, and I couldn't get it through the house without my mom figuring out what I was going to do.

I gathered my bow and arrows and was about to leave when I noticed the locker was open. I looked inside and saw my dad's collection of guns. He had three pistols, four rifles, and a shotgun. I pulled out a .22 rifle and decided to leave my bow behind. At the bottom of the locker was a stockpile of ammo, and I filled my coat pocket with .22 rounds. I hadn't fired the other guns, so I didn't really know how to use them, and they would have been useless to me.

I led Judy out of the stall and walked her carefully towards the back gate. It was going to be touch and go for a minute, but I think it could be done. Our back gate locked automatically when it closed, so all I had to do was to close it after us once we got out. I tied a string to the top and held the end as I got on top of Judy. She was a good horse and tolerant of boys, so she didn't try to bite me as I got on her bare back. I stayed low and covered myself with one of her blankets. I was trying to make myself part of the scenery, and as far as I knew, the Trippers never attacked animals. For some reason, they never considered them as threats.

I reached out and pulled the gate open just enough to let Judy pass. As we slipped out, I pulled on the string, closing the gate behind us. The click of the latch was loud, and I could hear shuffling and grunting as the Trippers came to investigate. I nearly screamed as several of them touched the horse, and their hands slid along the blanket that was covering me. If any of them grabbed it and pulled it off, it was going to go very badly.

I nudged Judy forward, guiding her mostly by instinct, and letting her pick her own way. She knew the terrain and the path we used to get over to the woods, so it wasn't all that difficult. She bumped Trippers out of the way, and under my blanket I could see some of them as they stumbled and fell away from her.

We kept moving, and I had to resist the urge to look back or try to see something. I knew they were all around me, and I knew they were going to go nuts once I activated the other part of my plan, but I had no other way to get so many Trippers away from the house. I couldn't just try and kill them all, and I wasn't tall enough to do what my dad had done, so this was the next best plan.

Judy's pace picked up as she crossed the old road and stepped into the ditch on the other side. I dared to look up a bit and guide her along. I nearly fell off as we climbed the steep side of the dam, and only by grabbing a double handful of mane did I stay where I was.

Once we reached the top, I was sure it was safe to take the blanket off. I flipped it off and took a look around. From my vantage point, I could see hundreds of Trippers surrounding our house and the houses around ours. There were many over by Trey's, and I could also see several dead ones, so I knew Trey's dad had been busy.

I also saw some activity by my house. The back door opened, and my mother walked out. She was wearing just a tee-shirt and jeans, which was unusual since the weather was turning cold. She looked up at me, and I actually raised a hand to her. She raised one back, and then walked to the back gate. I had another really bad feeling, and I started to turn Judy when my feeling came true.

My mom opened the gate, stepped through, and closed it behind her. It took about three seconds for the Trippers to notice her, and I could do nothing to save her.

CHAPTER 27

The first one to reach her jumped on her, bringing her to the ground. After that I couldn't see anything but bloody fists rising and falling. I couldn't breathe, I couldn't yell. All I could do was watch my mother walk out to be beaten to death.

Finally, after a minute, the Trippers stood up and milled about again. There was a broken shape on the ground completely covered in red.

My voice returned in a few seconds, and Judy nearly reared in surprise as my yell echoed out across the trees and small valley.

"*Noooooo!*" I screamed in anger and fear and frustration. I didn't know what to do, but I was nothing but raw emotion. I couldn't think; all I could do was grip Judy's mane until my knuckles were white.

If I had thought the Trippers were just going to be satisfied with helping my mother with her suicide, I was seriously mistaken. My outburst caused a couple of hundred infected heads to turn my way, and when they saw me sitting on my horse on top of a hill, they let out a collective yell and hurried my way.

For my part, I was ready. I brought Judy over to a small bus which was located next to a fallen log. I picketed her and let her munch on the bush while I ran over to the edge of the hill and set up a spot to shoot Trippers. I stuck a forked stick in the ground, making a rest for the rifle. I figured to get as many as I could before they gained the top. I knew the steep hill would slow them down, although if they decided to go up the road a bit I was in for a long day.

The first Trippers made the hill in good time, and they were about halfway up before I was fully ready. I loaded the tube of the rifle and placed the gun on the rest. My first target was a female, about fifteen years old with deep red splotches on her face and bite marks on her shoulder. Her hands dripped blood, and I knew she was one of the ones who had killed my mother. I lined up the sights on her eyes and pulled the trigger. The high velocity round caught her in the left eye and killed her instantly, dropping her onto the hill and tumbling her down a few paces. Her body caught up the legs of other Trippers, slowing them down as they tried to climb the hill and over her body.

I fired until the gun clicked on empty, and I reloaded as quickly as I could. The bodies I had piled up were causing a delay on the rest of the monsters climbing the hill which bought me the time I needed. I slipped the tube spring back into place and charged the rifle, placing it back on the rest for my next round of firing.

I reloaded that rifle six times, and killed a Tripper with nearly every shot. If my math was right, I had accounted for about eighty of the bastards. Not a bad reckoning for my mother.

As I was bringing the rifle up for the seventh time, I saw the Trippers were moving towards the west, getting around the firing line. That was my signal to go. They were going to flank me soon, and that would be all for me.

I whistled for Judy, and the good girl lifted her head and whinnied, pawing at the ground. I ran like the wind and skidded to a stop next to the animal. The log I tied her next to was still in the right spot, and I used it to quickly get on her back. I leaned far forward and yanked her picket rope out of the ground, gathering up the reins. I kicked her in the sides and whispered loudly, "Go, girl! Go!"

God bless her, Judy took off. She raced down the back of the earthen dam, and I had a time staying on her back. I wasn't the best rider, and the terrain wasn't level or even. But she stayed true and allowed me to pull her to a stop to see if we were being followed. We were standing next to a small creek that ran through the back prairie of the dam. There was a line of trees that grew along a small stream that led to the creek and tall grass that covered the area between the dam and the road out back. It was the same road Trey and I had taken to get to that one school that had given us so much trouble.

The Trippers were milling about the top of the dam, and finally one of them saw me out on the prairie. They howled and gave chase, falling on their faces in their rush to get out at me. About fifty of them were coming over the top of the dam, and nearly every one fell down as they rushed forward. I felt a pang in my chest as I thought about my mother, and tears filled my eyes as I watched the sick bastards stumble forward. It was too far away to line up a shot, so I started walking Judy away from the tangled mess of human disease. I rode her over to the road, and when there was enough distance between myself and the pursuing Trippers, I dismounted and removed her bridle and bit.

I rubbed her neck, and she brought her nose down to bump me in the chest.

I held her head tightly for a second before I looked into her big brown eyes.

"You have to run now, Judy. You have to go. I can't keep you with me. Go to the forest. Go south. You're free." I was talking to an animal that didn't understand me at all. "Go!" I shouted, and slapped her on the hindquarters as hard as I could.

That seemed to work. She bolted and ran down the road, then stepped into the woods on the south side. I figured she would be okay. I had no idea what to do with her, and I wasn't sure I could keep her with me. It was better she was off on her own. I figured she'd eventually wind up on someone's farm, which was fine.

I couldn't waste time worrying about it, though; the Trippers were still coming to get me.

CHAPTER 28

I ran to the gate of the subdivision on the other side of the road. All of the houses here had been abandoned a long time ago, and anything of value or use had been taken. The only real redeeming feature of this collection of houses was the solid fence that ran along the northern border. That was going to be what saved me. It was nine feet tall and a foot and a half wide at the top and made out of brick and mortar. It would have made a great barrier to the waves of Trippers, but the problem was it was only on two sides of the community. That fact made it useless against waves. But for now, it was going to be just what I needed.

I ran to the iron gate and climbed up onto the top of the fence. Once there, I waited until the Trippers were coming over the road before I did anything about it. I was seated on a decorative light, probably eleven or twelve feet above the ground. Just high enough to be out of reach of the tallest Tripper.

I loaded my rifle and made sure I had my ammo within easy reach. I thought I had enough to deal with the last of this crowd, but it might be close.

The infected horde came loping over, and when they hit the wall beneath me they raised their heads in fury at the interloper in their territory. I used their eyes as targets and punched holes in their heads. Fifteen dropped to my rifle in thirty seconds, and the noise infuriated the rest. They pushed forward, punching each other and elbowing one another out of the way. I didn't feel anything as I pulled the trigger; I was just getting rid of the trash of my world.

After a couple of minutes, and about thirty Trippers later, I noticed they were getting higher. I realized they were standing on their fallen comrades, but their footing was unsteady. Several times I missed due to a diseased person slipping and dodging the bullet at the right time.

Ten minutes later I was alone on the prairie. The ground in front of me was a small pyramid of corpses. I had no way of lighting them up, so they were going to have to have an open grave.

I dug into my pocket to get some more bullets to reload the rifle with, and I came out with three rounds. That was it. I had only three rounds left to see me back to my house. Oh, hell. I actually shook a bit as I realized what that actually meant.

I slipped off the fence and ran as fast as I could down the road. I needed to get into familiar territory if I wanted to have a chance of surviving. Even though I had killed a lot of Trippers, there was no way of knowing if they all were gone or if some were waiting behind. Trippers did that sometimes; they were very unpredictable.

I slid into the woods on the north side of Laraway Road, and I was much more at home here. I knew this small section of timber as well as I knew my backyard. I knew the trails and the hiding places and hoped both would see me home.

Home. I thought about my mother, and the tears started again. I don't know what made me feel worse. The thought that my mother was dead or the thought that I was truly alone now. I had no family anywhere. I stopped moving through the brush as the feeling overwhelmed me, and I sat down next to a big tree to try and settle the empty feeling in my gut.

I must have nodded off, because when I looked up again the sun had nearly set. The Trippers would be very active in this area, and the chances of me getting home were very slim. I had led dozens into this area, and even though I had killed a bunch, there were likely a lot roaming around here that I didn't get. Right about now I felt stupid for leaving the house. I felt guilty when I thought that, because I wondered if my mother would have stayed in the yard had I stayed home to stop her.

I couldn't stay here; the nights were getting very cold as winter began pushing fall out of the way. I had to try to get home. Hopefully in the dark I could make it. I moved quietly away from the tree and moved slowly north. I could see but just barely. Dusk was here, and the light sky against the dark ground made it hard to see details.

My hearing was fine, though, and I distinctly heard something moving behind me. I looked back but couldn't see anything. I tried to move faster, but it was hard when I was trying to be silent, too.

I passed my regular game trails and traps and made my way to the trail that took me to the top of the dam. I didn't want to try and cross the mess of dead bodies on the hill, so I had to go west a bit and get out that way. That meant going deeper into the woods and giving whatever was following me a better chance at catching up.

"Damn." That was all I had to say about that. I moved down the trail, and there was a crashing sound behind me as something big pushed through the underbrush. Twigs and branches snapped loudly in the gloom, and I whipped out my knife to face whatever was behind me. But the noises stopped, and I decided to use the silence to run like hell.

I ran quickly, cursing as branches smacked me in the face and legs. One big one actually tripped me up a bit, but I kept moving. Behind me, I could hear whatever it was moving with me and getting closer. By the sound of it, there may have been two of them.

I reached what I thought was the turn to get out of the woods, but I found myself blocked by one of the huge sticker bushes that lined the road. There was no way I was getting through that. If this thing was here, then I overshot the opening.

I whispered to myself out of frustration. "Dammit! Idiot!" I shut up as the steps following me came closer. I tried to calm myself, but my heart was racing and the blood was roaring in my ears. I held my knife the way my dad had taught me, but that was the only thing I could remember from his training. I sunk back into the bush as well as I could, and I could feel the stickers grabbing at my clothes. I'd be a mess if I had to get out of here in a hurry. My only hope was to try and become part of the scenery and hope whatever it was following me would pass me by.

Long minutes of waiting were rewarded by the sound of footsteps getting closer and closer. The Tripper, which is what I knew it had to be, stepped forward carefully, putting one step slowly in front of the other. I had never seen a Tripper stalking anyone, but then, why not? It knew I was here somewhere.

In the darkness, I could see a huge shape emerge from the woods. I almost screamed when I saw how bit it was. It had to be over six feet tall, closer to seven. It moved slowly, checking the ground and coming closer and closer. I held the knife and waited for the right moment to strike. I was only going to get one chance.

It came closer and closer, heading right for me. I wondered then if the rumors were true that the Trippers could actually see better in the dark than they could during the day. If that was true, then there wasn't any point in hiding anymore.

Suddenly it was on top of me. Something pushed me in the chest, and I fell deeper into the bush. My arm got tangled, and my knife was useless. I closed my eyes and waited for the beating to begin.

Something velvety pushed itself onto my face, and a large exhaling of breath in my face made me laugh out loud. My attacker retreated slightly at the noise, then came back to push me again.

I reached out with my free arm and ran a grateful hand up and down the long face of my dad's faithful horse.

"Judy, you scared the living shit out of me," I said.

CHAPTER 29

Thanks to Judy, my problem of getting back into the yard was solved. I just did the same thing I had done when I had left. The hard part was trying not to look at the bloody mess that once had been my mother, and thankfully the darkness hid the worst of that. It wasn't going to be pleasant in the morning.

Once inside the gates, I led Judy to the garage, not wanting her to be out in the shed all by herself. There weren't nearly as many Trippers as there was before, and hopefully in the morning I would be able to dispose of the rest. I gave Judy an extra helping of feed and made sure she had plenty of water. Afterwards, I went inside.

The quiet of the house overwhelmed me, and I spent the next hour or so crying and trying to figure out what I was going to do. For the first time in my life, I was completely alone.

I woke up shivering on the floor in the living room. The fire had gone out a long time ago, and I must have dozed off in between feeling sorry for myself and being angry at the world. It wasn't fair I was by myself. I hated my mother for being so selfish, then I felt guilty for hating her. I was so mixed up I didn't know what to do.

"Just keep moving, just keep busy," I said aloud. It was the only thing I could think of. If I stayed busy, I wouldn't have time to think about the horrible turn that my life had suddenly taken. What was I supposed to do? What was I supposed to become? I didn't know. I didn't know anything.

I fed myself and Judy, then took a shovel to dig another grave by my father. I spoke to him as I dug, telling him about my adventure in the woods and Mom's suicide. If I thought I was going to get some sort of sign about what I was supposed to do now, I must have missed it.

The sun was high when I finally worked my way over to where my mother's body lay. I had checked out the area from the second floor of the house, and the Trippers seemed to have moved on.

With any luck, they'll find a well-populated town that will kill them quickly.

I opened the gate and looked around. On the ground about ten feet from the fence was my mom. She was lying on her back with one arm covering her face and the other outstretched away from her. She looked like she was just out taking a nap, not lying there dead.

I pulled her arm away and her face was peaceful, almost serene. Her neck was one big wound that had bled out all over the ground. At least she died somewhat quickly, and they hadn't beaten her to death.

I stretched out the tarp I had brought with me, and without much ceremony, I rolled my mother onto it. Grabbing two ends, I slid her along the ground, stopping only to walk back and lock the gate. When we reached her grave, I pushed her in, burying her in loose dirt and rocks. The way I figured it, my parents could argue the merits of their actions for a long time to come.

Winter was on its way, and if I wanted to survive I was going to have to be ready. Looking over our stores, I saw that I was stocked pretty good with canned stuff; mom must have worked hard to get some stuff ready before Dad and she died. With only myself to feed, I think I was going to be okay. There were always rabbits around in the winter, and with the cold they would keep a lot longer. I would have to set up some traps closer to the house so I wouldn't be hiking through the snow to look for food.

During the last two winters, we had some interesting visitors. Dad had said he had never seen them this far south before, but if the weather was cold enough north, then they might find easier pickings to the south. But if this was a cold winter, and all signs said it was going to be, then they would be back.

I only saw them at dusk when the sky was light but the land was dark. They were grey ghosts that misted through the trees, stalking and watching. I had never seen wolves in the flesh before, and I thought they were dogs at first. But Dad had set me straight. They were the biggest wolves he had ever heard of, and they could easily take a horse down if they wanted to. He said some breeder's stock must have gotten free and were roaming the northern woods. We waited in the house for them to move on, and even when my dad had taken a shot at one of them, they just looked at us in calm contempt. I hoped they would stay north.

I spent a week getting in a supply of wood for the stove and feed for the horse. I kept myself as busy as possible, trying not to think about how quiet the house was and how alone I was. I went over to Trey's house a couple times, and Trey's mom was sad to hear about my mother, but that was about it. They invited me to live with them, but I knew I couldn't. They had enough mouths to feed, and one more wouldn't help them this winter. I think they were relieved when I refused.

During the evenings I practiced with my Colt and practiced my fighting skills. I was getting stronger and getting faster in pulling it out of my holster. I reasoned that being able to shoot quickly in a crisis might make the difference between being alive and being dead. Besides, I had my westerns to feed my imagination about becoming a gunfighter.

After a couple of weeks, I felt I had enough wood for the house for the winter. I had filled the back porch, and I had filled in the attic space above the garage with feed for Judy. If I ever found a cat that liked me, I was going to keep it to get the mice that liked living up there.

CHAPTER 30

Trey came by on a cold day about ten days after I had finished my work. He had stayed away on the advice of his father, figuring I needed time to work things through. But Trey had become bored and figured we'd get out one more time before the first serious snows.

"Hey Josh! What's your day look like?" Trey said, smiling like he had a secret.

I thought for a second. "Well, I figured I'd find out what a certain friend of mine was doing, and if it wasn't too stupid, I'd tag along to keep him out of trouble."

"Oh, you did, did you?" Trey said, eyeballing me like he wanted to hit me.

"What's on your mind?" I asked, not wanting to get into a fight.

"Let's head over to Frankfort. I've a mind to see a town."

I was slightly surprised. "Isn't that the town that you said you wanted to stay away from; that they took your knife and wouldn't give it back?"

Trey looked at me funny. "Oh, no, that was another town further west. What do you say?"

I hadn't been to a town in years and was curious. I thought about stuff I might have to trade and realized that the only goods I had of any value would be the guns in my father's locker.

"All right. We walking or riding?" I asked.

"In this cold? Hell, no. We're riding. I'll go get Pumpkin saddled and be back in a minute." Trey was so excited, he fairly jumped out of the house.

I smiled at my friend's enthusiasm and saddled Judy up in no time. She seemed to be eager to get out of the confines of her stall in the garage, and I needed her out of there as well, since I needed to clean that place up. The manure we always piled up around the base of the fence. My dad figured it might keep the Trippers away of they smelled only animal smell.

Once Judy was saddled I went upstairs to get a coat. My Dad's barn coat was still hanging on the pegs by the door. I took it down and shrugged it on. It fit better that I thought it would, being that my dad had been a big man. The sleeves were too long, and it hung to my knees, but I wanted to wear it anyway.

I put my knife on my belt, and as an afterthought, I put my Colt on as well. I had gotten used to its weight by wearing it around the house whenever I could, and I still practiced drawing it and "point shooting" like my dad had taught me.

I went to the gun locker and looked things over. The shotgun could be useful in hunting for birds, so I left that there. The rifles included the .22, but it had cleared a horde, so it had proven its worth. There was a bolt-action rifle in there with a scope on it, something I had never seen Dad use, along with a very heavy single shot rifle. Tucked in the corner was a small carbine, and as I drew it out, I knew it was love at first sight. It was a lever action rifle; the kind I had been reading about for years. The name on the barrel said 'Winchester', and it was chambered in .45 Colt. I nearly let out a little squeal when I saw that, since it shared the same ammo as my Colt.

"Meant to be," I said, holding that gun. I put it back, but this time in the front.

The three handguns weren't of much interest to me, since I had my Colt, but there were two I would keep. My father's police gun—the one he used when he was an officer—and the one he had said belonged to his father, my grandfather, who I had never met. That one was a revolver like mine but different. I'd have to look at it later, not now. The last handgun was one I figured I could trade. It was a boxy looking thing, and a quick scan of the ammo told me I had no bullets for it.

"Meant to be again," I said. I put the gun in my pocket, and just as I did, Trey came bouncing back into the garage.

"Ready to go, man?" Trey looked at me and suddenly cocked his head to the side for a second.

"What?" I asked, wondering what joke he was going to make. I put a hand on my coat sleeve self-consciously.

"Nothing. You just look like your dad in that coat. Sorry, man." Trey seemed somewhat embarrassed to have brought it up.

"No worries. Let's get going before it gets too late," I said, swinging up onto Judy. She seemed ready to move and was eager to get out. Trey bounded out to Pumpkin, and together we started up the road. We moved the horses at a quick walk, taking them down around the bend where the dark house was. I stared intently at the windows, but nothing looked back at me. Even now I wondered if it all was just part of my imagination.

I was armed with my Colt, and if I knew Trey, he had one of his father's guns on him. Trey's father was a trusting man, but his trust only went so far when it came to his son.

The road stretched out before us and we moved along at a decent pace. The horses were happy to be out, and they took to the trail eagerly. As we moved along old Sauk Trail, named after the Saulk Indians who used to live here sometime way before I cared, the world seemed like a relatively normal place. The houses we passed seemed like they were still lived in, and the roads seemed like they were just waiting for the crowds to come home, like they did a long time ago. The church, used once as a refuge from the Trippers, shone brightly in the morning sun, the cold clear air making everything stand out in sharp contrast.

We crested a hill and started working our way down towards the valley. There was a creek that ran through here; the same one that ran behind mine and Trey's houses. It collected in a wide pond at the bottom of the valley, and then wound its way south, heading off to some larger body of water, I'm sure. The pond was ringed on the north side by huge oak trees, and the southern end was bare except for a small hill that was cleared of trees. At the top of the hill was a trio of wooden crosses. I didn't know what to make of that.

The bridge that crossed the creek was full of holes, and both Trey and I walked our horses over, making sure they stepped carefully. I sure didn't want to lose Judy because she broke her leg stepping in a stupid hole.

As we walked toward the other side, Judy suddenly jerked on her reins. Pumpkin reared as well, and it took all of Trey's strength and mine to calm the horses down.

"Dammit!" Trey yelled, trying to control his horse. "They're trying to run home!"

"If they run across that bridge, they'll break their legs for sure," I said, pulling hard on the reins and trying to drag Judy over to the side of the road. If she bolted from there, at least she would head for decent ground, and I could catch her in the woods.

Trey and I led the horses away from the bridge, and they seemed to calm down the further we left the road. I noticed the change and saw that Trey had noticed it as well.

"Something on the side of the road?" he asked.

I nodded. I also noticed he put his hand on his coat as if to reassure himself that something was still there. If I was a betting man, I'd say that was where Try had put his gun. "We'd better deal with it," I said. "We have to come this way on the return trip, and those two won't act any better."

"Got that right. That horse jumped at a squirrel once and knocked over a whole barrel of water. Flooded the damn basement," Trey said, throwing a look of disgust at the horse. "But she's the best runner we got, so she comes with."

"All right, let's go look. Maybe it's just a dead animal," I said with a confidence I really didn't feel. I slipped the little loop of leather off the hammer of my Colt, and loosened it in its holster. Trey noticed it and slipped a hand under his coat as well.

When I reached the road, I listened very carefully, trying to see if there was any sound there that wasn't supposed to be. That was a trick my dad taught me, and in this particular case, it was a trick that was completely useless. The creek babbled enough over a series of rocky steps that it was impossible to hear anything trying to sneak up on us.

Stepping onto the road, I looked back at the horses, and they were both staring at us as we stood on the trail. Their ears were up, and they were flicking their tails nervously. Something was here, all right.

"*Josh!*" Trey screamed.

CHAPTER 31

I turned back to the road just in time to see a grey shape leap at me from the woods. All I could see was a blood red mouth filled with fangs hurtling at me at incredible speed.

I tried to step out of the way, and there was a terrific noise that shattered the peace of the valley. A sudden bark rushed past my head, and a huge paw slapped me on the shoulder, knocking me down. I fell back and groped for my gun, surprising myself that it was already in my hand. I thought that was kind of strange.

"Holy shit! Holy shit! Jesus Christ and Holy Shit! Josh, are you okay? Man! I never thought I would ever see anything like that. Damn, that's a big animal," Trey said in a rush.

I looked over at my assailant and saw that it was a huge wolf. I scrambled to get back away from it and held my gun out, ready to take a shot at it. I figured Trey had already shot it once, but I wasn't taking chances. As I got to my feet, I realized Trey was still talking to me.

"How did you do that? I never saw anybody pull a gun that fast," he said excitedly.

"What are you talking about?" I asked as I looked over the beast. It was at least six feet long and looked like it had fed pretty well the last few weeks. Its fur was glossy, and its flanks were full.

"You shot that wolf as it jumped," Trey said. "I didn't even see your hand move. Suddenly you were shooting."

I looked down at the gun in my hand and saw that it had indeed been fired. I replaced the spent cartridge with a new one, and put the gun back in its holster. I didn't remember drawing and firing; all I could remember was that mouth full of teeth flying at me from the edge of the woods.

I shrugged as I turned to Trey. "Must have been all that practice I've been doing since I've got nothing else to do."

Trey looked at me kind of sideways, like he wasn't really sure how he was supposed to take my answer. I always got defensive when he did that.

"It's true!" I said. "Once Judy's been fed and I've checked my lines and cut the wood I need, what else do I have to do besides practice what my dad taught me? No one needs me for anything." My voice trailed off, and I felt a little lump start in my chest. The last thing I wanted was to have Trey see anything that looked like a tear in my eyes.

Trey nodded. "Yeah, I can see that. Well, for what it's worth, that practice paid off. "He changed the subject. "We gonna skin him or what? That pelt might be worth something."

I looked at the sky. "May as well. If we get it to town, we can trade it before we have to tan it," I said. "You want to skin it or make a travois? No way Pumpkin or Judy is going to haul anything on their backs that smells like wolf or blood. Or both."

Trey sighed. "I'll skin it. You're too quick with skinning and would make a mess of it anyway. Go find some poles."

I walked carefully into the woods, keeping my hand near my gun. Wolves weren't usually loners unless they were juveniles, and this one was too big for that. If he wasn't the alpha, he was darn close to it. The rest of the pack may be close or may be far, it was too difficult to tell. Either way, we'd be gone before they came through again.

I found two saplings that would serve, and quickly cut them down and stripped them of their branches, saving the longer ones. As I walked back towards the horses, I took branches off other trees, trying to make sure they were the same size.

I passed Trey skinning the wolf, and he was having a time getting the skin off the shoulders. I would have offered to help, but he would have refused. We both knew it, so there was no point in bothering. He was actually doing a good job of keeping the blood off himself and the rest of the pelt, so this may turn out easier than I had hoped.

I rigged the travois onto Judy since she was the younger of the two horses. The longer poles I slid through the stirrups and tied them in place with a small piece of rawhide string. I wove the branches into a small mat and tied it to the poles. It wasn't the best I could do, but since we were only travelling a few more miles, it would get the job done.

Trey had the wolf skinned by the time I was finished, and I helped him load the pelt. It was still a little bloody, but then so was Trey. Pumpkin bucked a little when she smelled the coppery stink on Trey. Judy was not very happy having to haul the wolf skin, and I was waiting for her to let her feelings be known. As we walked, her ears were flat back at me, and I knew it was a matter of time before she tried something.

We walked up what was left of the road and passed out of the small valley. A brick house was on the left side of the road at the top of the hill. Old trees lined the yard, and tall grass waved gently in the breeze. There wasn't any fence around the yard, yet the house seemed tight and secure.

"Think anyone's home?" I asked Trey.

"Go look if you want to," Trey said. "That place looks creepy."

Trey was right about that. The house set back on its yard like it was waiting for something to enter its lair. The layout of the small ranch was in the shape of an 'L', with the door at the intersection. Trees in the back yard leaned over the house casting a gloom over the whole section. Shadows of the branches extended over the front of the building like long fingers waiting for something to come within reach.

"Well, if you're too scared, I figure I can wait until you're not here to hold me back," I said.

"Oh, you think so?" Trey said. He swung his leg around and got off Pumpkin.

Before I could think of a decent retort, Trey was stomping through the yard, walking directly towards the door. He picked up a branch and used it to pound on the door.

"Hey! Creepy house! Anybody home?" Trey banged the door a few more times then threw the branch away. He snapped his fingers then walked back through the yard, grinning at me the whole time.

I nodded, giving Trey his due. I wouldn't have gone up to the door, and I was the one who had just killed a wolf with a fast draw.

CHAPTER 32

We rode past the house, leaving the creepiness behind. The road curved to the north, and we passed two homes on the right side of the road. One of them was occupied as evidenced by the triple deep wooden fence around the yard and the three horses who came over to say hello to our mounts. We didn't stick around, because the smell of the pelt spooked the small herd, and I didn't want trouble with the owners for raising a ruckus.

The other house was quiet, with the door open wide. I figured there was nothing there even to salvage, so we just kept riding.

"Oh, shit. Company," Trey said. He pointed to the house we just passed.

Stumbling out of the front door was a Tripper. He was about the same age as my dad and looked like he had seen better days. His clothes were threadbare and full of holes, and he looked like he had cut his face on something a while ago. A long gash ran from his chin to nearly his ear, punctuating the blotches on his face.

He wheezed loudly, and both horses jumped a bit, looking to run away. I led Judy away a bit, keeping her under control, and Trey followed along. The Tripper was working his way towards the road, and pretty soon he was going to be moving a lot faster.

"We gonna run, shoot, what?" Trey asked, looking over his shoulder.

"I want to try something," I said. "If it doesn't work, you can shoot him."

"What do you mean, I can shoot him? I ain't got no gun," Trey said.

"Your dad didn't make you pack a gun?" I asked, not really believing him.

"Not this time. He said I didn't need it," Trey replied.

"Man, did he miss the day," I said, pulling my bow from its scabbard. I dismounted, quickly strung it, and then drew an arrow out. I walked away from the horses and waited for the Tripper. I figured if I missed, I would just shoot him in the head. I didn't like the thought of using up another bullet, but if it was him or me, I'd rather it be him.

It didn't take long; he came out of the yard and stumbled through the ditch, trailing bits of his clothing as burrs and weeds pulled at him. I waited for him to steady himself before I drew back on the bow. I wanted to make this first shot count and needed him to be mostly steady.

He came right at me, his face twisting in a mask of rage as his diseased brain saw me as a threat. His hands alternated between claws and fists, and his eyes burned red. If he were to get his hands on me, he'd do his best to tear me apart.

I never gave him the chance. When he was about fifteen yards away I loosed my arrow, sending it into his chest with a meaty thump. The Tripper took three steps towards me then stopped. He still reached out towards me, but he slowly sank to his knees. He tried to take a step, but he wound up falling forward, snapping my arrow underneath him.

I looked back at Trey who was deep in thought about what he had seen. I advanced on the Tripper, pulling my gun and keeping it trained on him. When I was close enough, I reached out with my bow and pushed him over onto his back. My arrow, splintered as it was, stuck out from the man's chest. There wasn't much blood, as Trippers never bled much, but I expected more than a small circle around the entry hole.

"Dead?" Trey asked.

"Looks like it," I said. I took another small rope and looped it around the Tripper's foot, dragging the dead man into the ditch. Eventually he'll serve as food for the crows and coyotes as soon as they figure out he's here. I went back to Judy, unstrung my bow, and remounted.

Trey and I rode on, being careful not to lose our pelt when we went over the rail road tracks that marked the boundary of the town of Frankfort.

As we walked in, Trey and I talked about the Tripper.

"Any thoughts?" I asked.

Trey shook his head. "None that make any sense. I've seen Trippers walking around with bullet holes in their chests, same as you."

"I know," I said. "And we can't be the first ones to see this happen."

"My dad says back in the day people were trying to kill these guys all kind of ways. Somebody had to put some sort of weapon besides a bullet through them," Trey said.

"I don't know. It's just strange." I said. "It's like the bullets go through the heart, and it's all good. But the arrow stays there, messing things up."

Trey thought about it. "Well, I'll say this. Until we know for sure, let's stick with the head shots."

"Deal."

We rode through the outskirts of what used to be the town of Frankfort. It was a small town with a good collection of homes. Several of them were reinforced, but it looked like most of them had been abandoned, looted a long time ago. We rode down the main street into town, and as we did we could see signs of violence.

Several homes had their fences breached, and the doors and windows were broken and open. There were dead animals lying about, and we could see dark shapes still lying on the floor where they fell under the Trippers' teeth and fists.

Trey spoke first. "Not sure I'm liking this much anymore, Josh."

"It's fine. We can get rid of this pelt and then head back. Just keep your bow handy," I said with a confidence I really didn't feel.

We moved further into town and saw more people. But they were not people who acted like they were residents of the town. These people were going into homes, pulling things out, putting things in carts and wagons, and then moving on to the next house. This was looting on a grand scale, and more than one of them looked at the two of us with more than passing interest.

I could understand that. We were essentially two boys riding very valuable animals. Pumpkin was a good walker, and anyone with an eye could see that Judy was a fine horse.

"Hey, boy! Boy! You on the horse!"

I reined in Judy and looked down at the man who was yelling at me. He was a short man, barely taller than I would have been had I been on the ground, and was wearing dirty clothing. A small cap held back his greasy hair from his face, and his left eyelid twitched when he spoke.

"What do you want?" I asked. Under my breath I whispered to Trey. "Keep an eye on our backs."

"Your horse looks like a fine animal. Would you sell him?" the man asked, stepping closer. I could see one of his hands, but not the other, and I didn't like it.

"No, she's not for sale. The pelt is, if you're interested in buying that," I said, keeping my eye on the man. I slid my right hand up to the top of my thigh, keeping it close to my gun.

The man looked at the pelt. "Hmm. No thanks. But I like your horse. If you're interested in selling or trading, you just let me know first, you hear?"

"I won't; thank you though. Come on, girl." I gave Judy a little nudge and she walked smartly away. When we reached the next block, I spoke in low voice to Trey.

"Think he'll leave us alone?" I asked.

"No, we'll probably see more of them before we leave. Man, I sure thought this was a good idea when I first came up with it," Trey said, more to himself than me.

"Well, you're more wrong than right anyway, so this ain't so bad," I said. I chuckled as an acorn whistled past my ear.

We reached the center of town and there were several shops and places of business. I went looking for a tanner while Trey stayed with the horses. On the edge of the central square there was a small building. I could see several pelts hanging on frames, stretching as they dried. I recognized several rabbits, a few deer, and there was even a large cow hide.

Inside the shop was a large assortment of hides, and I was grateful to see there weren't any wolf pelts. Perhaps we could get more in trade.

"Help you, son?" the man behind the table of pelts asked. He was working with some leather on a belt, adding some decoration with a hammer and some punches.

"I have a pelt to sell or trade," I said, picking up a length of stiff leather. It was tanned black, which really looked nice.

"What kind of pelt?" the man asked with a sigh. "I already have plenty, as you can see. But, since I know your dad, I'll make you a fair offer, no matter what it is."

"You know me?" I asked, perplexed.

"Everyone around here does. You're Josh Andrews, and your old man is the law around here. He's a good man; helped me out several times." The man smiled, and stood up. "Where's your dad?" he asked. "Hope he's out there taking care of those drifters."

I shook my head. "My father's dead. Tripper bit him a while back," I said quietly as the memories came back all of a sudden.

The tanner sighed deeply. "That would explain a lot. You any good with that gun under your coat?" he asked suddenly.

I started slightly. "I killed the wolf with it," I said defensively.

The man nodded. "You're too young to be the law yourself, but maybe in a few years? We'll see. Let's take a look at that pelt."

We walked outside and over to where Trey was waiting. There was a small group of men who seemed to be deep in conversation across the green where we had the horses, but they didn't seem to be interested in us at the moment.

In the end, we managed to trade the pelt for a new gun belt and holster for myself, and a new knife for Trey. I traded the old pistol for a couple of boxes of 45 Colt ammunition. Apparently I was the only one around who had a gun for it. I was thinking about being able to shoot the rifle chambered for that caliber as well.

CHAPTER 33

We rode out of town, following the same way we came in. The drifters were still at work, only this time we knew more about who they were. The tanner told us that the drifters were nomads who followed the Trippers, looting homes after the diseased walkers had moved on. They didn't do anything but take what other people had gathered, going in when it was safe. They were little better than Trippers themselves. Sometimes they finished what the Trippers had started. It was rumored that the drifters killed the survivors if they were weak enough.

We passed the man who wanted to buy Judy earlier, and this time he just looked at me. I held his stare until I had passed, keeping a hand near my gun. If my father had been here, he'd probably have forced that crowd to move on. I felt a wave of sadness sweep over me, and I struggled to keep it together. I knew if any of this crowd saw weakness, they'd follow me home. Deep down, I almost wished they would.

I didn't know what was coming over me. After losing my parents I was spiraling into a blackness I wasn't sure I wanted to get out of. Part of me wanted to crawl into a warm bed and cry myself to sleep every night, and the other part, the scarier part, wanted to just hunt down bad people and kill them.

I told Trey what I was thinking, since he was my only friend, and he gave it to me straight.

"Man, don't be stupid. You got every right to hate the Trippers for what they did. And you been using that anger to focus yourself on fighting them. It gave you something to do and probably will save your life someday. Hell, it already has," Trey said. He pulled out his new knife. "That wolf you killed would have torn us both apart. If you hadn't been working with that gun, he'd have been still eating us before killing our horses. You just need some more time to figure things out. It's going to be a long winter, and we're both going to be busy trying to survive it."

I had to admit, Trey was right. I was looking for some purpose, but maybe what I was supposed to do was just survive right now.

We crossed the tracks and started back towards the valley. The creepy house was still there, but the sun had shifted and lit up the back half of the house. The tree that had grown over the roof was grasping at the rear windows, and more than one branch looked like it was going to break the glass any week now.

I pulled Judy into the yard, and Trey followed.

"What are you doing? The sun is setting; we don't need to be out after dark. If you're going to prove you're as nervy as me, you're too late, man," Trey chided.

"I want to see if there's anything to read. I'm running out of material, and I'm not desperate enough for textbooks," I said, dismounting from Judy. I hit the ground and adjusted my gun belt. It hung lower than the one I had made, with the bottom of the holster nearly touching my knee. I took her lead rope and brought her close to the front door. If I had to get out in a hurry, I wanted her near.

"Man, I heard that," Trey said, getting off of Pumpkin. He led her over to the other side of the door. He shifted the knife on his belt, getting used to its heft and length. It was a camp knife, about seven inches worth of blade with a simple handle. It was longer and larger than anything Trey had before, and he was very pleased to have it.

I opened the front door and pushed it slowly aside. I stepped in slowly, trying not to make too much noise. The dust on the furniture and the floor told me this house had been abandoned for years, and I didn't see any footprints that would give away the presence of any Trippers.

"Quick sweep, see what we can find," I said.

"We looking for anything other than books?" Trey asked, stepping in beside me.

"I'm not, but you're welcome to whatever you find," I said. I took a look into the living room, but not seeing any books, I went into the first room I could find. It was a small bedroom with a made bed and two nightstands. There was a bookcase across from the bed, and I immediately went over to it.

"Jackpot," I said. I grabbed a dusty pillow off the bed and took the pillowcase off to use as a sack. I did that once before at my own house, and my mother gave me three kinds of hell for it. I checked the titles and nearly danced when I saw the first two rows were Louis L'Amour paperbacks. I transferred them to the sack and checked the rest of the titles. There were a few more westerns by Zane Grey and a bunch of things that looked like fantasy or science fiction. I grabbed them anyway, figuring a book was a book. On the bottom shelf there was a thick book, and I grabbed it. It was heavy, and I glanced at the title before I put it in the sack. The cover said The Lord of the Rings, whatever that meant.

Trey came walking out of the back bedroom with a sack of his own. "Found a bunch of romance novels. My mom will love me for this."

The sunlight was turning from gold to orange, and we needed to get out of the night or we were spending it here. We were about a half mile from the homesteads, and it was going to be a quick run. If the drifters were any indication, Trippers had been through this area recently and there might be stragglers.

We left the house closed up, and mounted our horses. They were not happy about the extra weight hanging from the saddle horn, but it shouldn't be long in getting home.

The setting sun was casting long shadows across the hilltops, and the valley we needed to go through was shrouded in grey. The shadows of the trees were dark on the ground, spotted with lighter shades of black and brown. The low area by the bridge was just one big dark shadow.

"Well, this is not how I was expecting the ride home to be," Trey said. "We *had* to look for books, didn't we?"

"What's the big deal? Ride through and we're done. Hell, the other entrance is right around that tree line," I said.

"Howdy boys!"

Judy started at the voice, and I had a time calming her down. I was grateful for the chance to hide my own shaken nerves. I never even looked down our back trail, and I cursed myself inwardly for not doing so.

"Jesus! What the hell is wrong with you?" Trey demanded, struggling to get Pumpkin under control.

The drifter from Frankfort had followed us out of town, and we had allowed him to get close—too close. He was leading two other men who were both armed with long sticks and what looked like ropes at their belts.

"Well, I decided I really liked the look of your horses, and figured I didn't really need to buy them after all. Both of you git down now afore you all git hurt." The man wasn't playing at nice now; he was all business.

Trey looked at me, and I looked at his horse and nodded.

"Hang on! They'll run if we try to get off now!" I said. I kept pulling the reins and giving Judy a kick on the side the men couldn't see. Trey was still having a hard time, and I could see him pulling on the reins as well. The horses whinnied and danced away from the men, who gave them a wide berth to calm down.

As soon as both horses were facing the road, I gave Judy her head and kicked her in the ribs. She shot out of that driveway like she was launched from a cannon, with Pumpkin right behind her. Trey and I rode low on our horses' necks, holding tight as we raced away.

All we heard from the men behind us was a startled "Hey!" I threw a quick glance behind me and saw the men were running after us. The men with ropes were running with them in hand, and I was worried if they got close enough they might get lucky and catch one of us in a loop.

We raced down the hill and reached the bottom of the valley where it leveled off before rising again. The bridge was the connection between the sides, and once we started up the other side, we'd leave the men far behind. The setting sun cast a deep shadow here, and it would be pitch black before long, and would stay that way until the moon came out and showed its face.

Suddenly Judy pulled up short, and I had a time settling here again. Pumpkin slid into us, and both Trey and I were hard put to settle the horses for real this time. I looked over at the bridge, and swore softly.

CHAPTER 34

"Shit!" I lay flat on Judy's back and prayed she didn't buck. Trey took his cue from me and did the same, rubbing Pumpkin's neck and whistling softly to her.

On the far side of the bridge there were four Trippers. I could barely see them in the gloom, but their pale skin stood out. They were walking down the road and would be upon us soon. In between the blowing of Judy's lungs, I could hear the wheezing of the infected people.

"Hey! Git back here! I gotta come down there, you ain't gonna like it!" The voice of the man from town echoed down the valley, bouncing off the trees and skimming across the water from the pond.

The Trippers reacted immediately, walking towards the sound and breathing heavier. Unfortunately, that meant they were headed right for us.

"Stay low. Be a part of your horse." I said softly. "Follow me." I turned Judy's head and nudged her with my knees, keeping low on her neck. I could feel her tension, but she stayed true and walked slowly off the road towards the hill on our left. The tall grass silenced her hooves, and I was relieved to see Trey was right behind me. We eased the horses and ourselves slowly through the grass, keeping the Trippers in sight as we let our horses walk away from trouble.

"Where the hell did you two git to, goddammit!" The voice came from lower down the hill. "Whut the hell? Oh, shit!"

The men who were after us must have found themselves face to face with the Trippers, and there was a lot of screaming after that. I heard one man scream he had been bit, another gave out a gurgling cry that ended abruptly, and there was the sound of running feet as one man abandoned his comrades and took off. I heard the meaty sound of a fist striking flesh over and over again, and a deep groan like someone was breathing out his last. If I had to guess, I'd say two men were dead and the third was bringing trouble back to wherever he had come from.

We crossed the small land bridge that separated the creek from the pond and made our way through the forest. Dark branches reached out and caressed our cheeks letting us know we were welcome to stay if we wanted to. Once upon a time there was a campground here, and we rode our horses past the abandoned buildings. These cabins would be useless for defense since they had no fence and were made of thin wood. The only building that might be worth using was the main lodge, but it had huge windows in the front which would be fine until the first Tripper put his head through it.

On the far side of the campground, we hit another wall of brush and trees, and we took a right turn at that obstacle. A hundred yards from there we trotted our horses up onto the road and continued home.

The entire time we spent in the woods Trey and I didn't say a word. We didn't know if there were any more Trippers about, and who wanted to bring them home with us?

"Damn," Trey said.

"No kidding," I replied. I gave Judy a reassuring pat on the neck, and she rewarded me by putting her ears back and arching her back a little.

We rode back to our houses, and by the time we reached them, it was fully dark. I made a circuit around the perimeter before going in, making sure there weren't any visitors I didn't want to have. I put Judy in the garage stall and gave her an extra bit of hay and fresh water. She'd earned it by keeping her cool.

Inside the house was quiet, cold, and dark. It reminded me in a big way that I was alone. I took my gun off and hung the new gun belt off the headboard of my bed. I figured the cowboys of old did it that way. The gun I lay on the side table, easy to hand if I needed it.

I took the books out of the pillowcase and arranged them on the top shelf of my bookcase. I had sixteen new westerns, ten fantasy books, and a few science fiction books. I was set for the winter.

I pulled out the big book, The Lord of the Rings, and hefted it. A book that weighed that much had to have some good material in there somewhere. I opened the book and jumped when something fell out and hit the floor with a metallic ring. I put the book down and felt around on the floor, eventually finding a heavy coin. I picked it up and held it to the candlelight.

It was a gold coin with a woman walking on the front and an eagle on the back. The words on the back said "1 ounce Fine Gold." I set it down and picked the book up again. Opening it carefully, I saw that the pages had been altered, allowing the gold coins to sit in the book without anyone being the wiser. I counted fifty gold coins in the book, along with fifty more silver coins.

Suddenly I had real wealth, and had no idea what to do with it. Disappointed I couldn't read the book, I put the fallen coin back, set the unusual bank on the shelf with its brethren, and promptly went to bed.

CHAPTER 35

The first serious snowfall hit us about a week later. You could smell it for almost half a day before it arrived. The flakes came down in groups and blanketed the cold ground almost immediately. I had spent the previous week gathering even more wood and laying in supplies, so I wasn't worried about being snowed in. If I didn't have Judy to care for, I probably wouldn't have gotten out of bed for much more than to eat and set another piece of wood in the stove. My dad had put small cast iron stoves in each of the bedrooms early on when the world fell apart. He knew the utilities would fail eventually and made sure we would survive the winters. The stoves sat on ceramic tiles and the pipes went directly out the side of the house. I don't remember dad installing them, as I was just a baby, but I was grateful these days for the thought he put into making sure his family survived. As I always did, I wished again to have him and my mom back.

I padded downstairs and checked on Judy. She was restless, so I led her outside, and let her walk around a bit. She danced a little in the snow and kicked a few flakes off of some of the bushes. She kept prancing around and shaking her mane, snorting as flakes got in her nose. I had to laugh, since she was acting like a long legged colt who was enjoying her first winter.

She finally came back in, and I spent a good hour rubbing her down. I cleaned out her stall and gave her some fresh hay for the day. I refilled her water trough, and just for fun I floated some snowballs in it. She spent a good ten minutes staring at those round balls of ice before she would take a drink, and even then she eyed the snow warily.

I went inside laughing at my silly horse and for a moment forgot how quiet everything was. I went back up to my room where the stove was happily consuming the oak log I had put in there, and I spent the rest of the morning and part of the afternoon in a deep dive into one of the westerns I had retrieved. I liked Louis L'Amour a lot, but that Zane Grey had a way with words that made you think.

The snow fell for the rest of the day, and it was nearly dark when it stopped. I had gone out to my traps and moved several of them closer and had gotten lucky with three of them. The rabbits I caught were still well-fed, so they would be good eating when I got around to them. I skinned the three and covered them with snow before I hung them outside. They'd keep for a good long time depending on how cold it got.

I practiced with my Colt for at least an hour each day. I wished I had the ammo to practice shooting it, but I only had a couple of boxes, and I had to be careful what I used those for. I had enough to fill the cartridge loops on the gun belt, and it held twenty-five. Trouble was, the extra weight again threatened to pull my pants down, so I had to make sure my belt was cinched tight.

I brought the guns from the garage into the house and put them in my closet. The Winchester I loaded with ten rounds and kept that near my bed as well. I read that cowboys did that, too.

The next day I spent a lot of time looking at my parent's clothes. I figured I would keep my dad's clothes, using them for myself as I grew up. I hoped to be as big as he was someday, but you never could count on things like that. I decided to give my mom's clothes to Trey's mother. She was about the same size as my mom, and she could wear them or make them fit her daughters, I didn't really mind which.

It had been about a week or so since Trey and I had been into town, and I wanted to see how they were doing. I figured I would go in the morning since it was late, and I was looking forward to burying myself under my new rabbit pelt blanket.

It was sometime really early in the morning when I awoke to hear a sound that didn't belong in the night. It was a scraping sound, like something was scratching at the gate, and then there was a clicking sound.

I sat up and quickly put on my shirt and pants. That was something my father had taught me. It was always better to walk into danger when you were dressed. For no other reason, it made you feel less exposed.

I picked up my gun, but then thought better of it and grabbed my bow. Even though I practiced drawing the Colt, I knew what I could do with my bow, and was confident of a kill shot at anything under seventy yards. I slipped my quiver over my shoulder and nocked an arrow as soon as I reached the ground floor. I looked out the window and saw a dark shape by the back gate. It was leaning over in the moonlight, holding the gate open with its body while it messed around with something on the ground. I watched for a second and saw that it was trying to prop the back gate open.

"What the hell?" I whispered as I eased open the kitchen window over the sink. It was the only window that opened with a crank instead of being pulled up, and it was the only window that was silent when I opened it.

The cold air crept in like a thief, and I felt it on my feet before I felt it on my arms. I drew back the arrow and aimed across the yard. I adjusted for the slight breeze from the west and let fly. The arrow streaked across the yard and hit what I figured to be a Tripper just below the shoulder in the back. The impact made a loud sound in the night, and the intruder hit the ground. In a flash it was up again, and running off into the darkness.

That was wrong. Trippers never ran. They walked fast, but their minds weren't capable of managing a run. What I hit was not a Tripper.

I went back upstairs and grabbed my rifle. I put my boots and coat on and went out into the yard. At the back gate, I saw some dark spots in the snow that were probably blood, but I couldn't be sure until daylight. I checked the gate and saw it was being propped open by a large branch. I pulled it out and closed the gate, securing the latch. If there were any Trippers around, they would have walked right through that gate and would have been a nasty surprise in the morning.

As I went back inside my somewhat warm house my head was spinning. I realized that all at once I had shot an uninfected person; the same person who had propped open my gate to try and get Trippers to kill me. That fact told me Trippers were in the area, and I nearly got the shakes when I thought I almost used my Colt to drive him off. That would have called every Tripper in the area right to my gate, which would have been open at the time.

CHAPTER 36

In the morning, I took my bow back outside with me, and together we went back to the rear gate. It was a brutally cold morning, and my face was already feeling numb. The sun was low in the sky, although the bright light was welcome. Everything was clear, even at a distance. A mist rose from the creek as the waters battled the ice trying to take over. It was a losing battle for the water. In a week or two, I was going to have to start making trips down to the water to make sure the pipe we had down there wasn't clogged or iced up. If the creek froze solid, I was going to have to go into snow melting for water, which would eat up my firewood.

Winter was a dangerous time to be outside. There wasn't any brush to hide behind except for the pine trees and holly bushes. The boxwoods stayed green, as did the pine bushes, but that was it. Any Tripper on a high place could see into homes and yards for a long way.

Sometimes I thought about leaving this area and heading south. My mom talked about the weather being better further south with winters not being so bad. But if I remembered my geography right, it was nearly a three-hundred-mile trip to the southern end of the state, and I didn't think I could manage it alone as a twelve-year-old.

I listened carefully before I opened the gate, and I kept an arrow ready for anything. I swung the gate wide, and before it was fully open, I could see the footprints of the intruder the night before. Outside the fence was a large depressed area where something had thrashed on the ground. I could see blood traces here and there, and there was a large arc of blood on the ground. My arrow was sticking out of the snow, which explained the blood. Whoever I had shot managed to rip the arrow out, and the blood followed the second flight of it. There were footprints heading off into the woods across the trail, and by the distance between the steps I figured whoever it was had been running pretty well. The prints were deep, which my dad always told me meant a bigger person.

I was so focused on reading the prints I nearly missed the Tripper who was plowing through the snow along my fence, heading right for me. There were three others behind him, and I was too far from my gate to make it back in time to close it.

He was a young man, probably around twenty, and he was pale from the cold, making the spots on his face stand out even more. His bloodshot eyes were locked on me, and his lips stretched back to reveal dark teeth as he advanced through the snow. His companions, a woman and two older men, saw me at the same time and started heading my way. Their wheezing breath split the quiet air and created mists around their heads.

I brought my bow up and released, aiming more by instinct than by sight. The arrow crossed the ten feet between us in an instant and transfixed the Tripper in his right eye, killing him instantly as the point cracked through his eye socket and pierced his brain.

I backed up as I drew another arrow, heading away from the open gate and my home. The three followed me, trying to get through the snow. I pulled my bowstring back and let another arrow go, this time hitting the second from the rear in the chest. He took two steps, stumbled to his knees, and then fell on his face. His last action drove the arrow out of his back.

I pulled another arrow out as I retreated, this time aiming for the woman who was closest to me. I shot her in the mouth as she opened it to scream at me, and the point made it all the way through the back of her head. She died with her eyes rolling up in her skull.

The last man came charging, and as I drew another arrow, I tripped over a log or root that was under the snow, and fell backwards. My bow and arrow were dropped as I tried to keep from falling on my back. The man kept coming, and I fumbled with my coat to get at my knife. I twisted around and managed to get to my feet, standing up to try and face the Tripper that was a foot taller than my five-foot-eight frame and at least fifty pounds heavier.

The man reached out to grab me, and just as I was ready to spin away, his forehead suddenly grew a broad head arrow point, the kind you usually find on a crossbow bolt. He fell on his face, and when he did I could see my very good friend Trey standing behind him with his crossbow. Trey's face was a mask of hate and rage, and as I watched he dropped his crossbow and brought his arm up to his eyes. That was when I realized Trey was crying.

CHAPTER 37

I picked up my fallen bow and arrow then went over to my friend.

"Trey, what's wrong man? You just saved my life!" I said, brushing the snow off my coat.

Trey gave a heaving sob. "They killed Trish, Josh! They killed her, and it was my fault!"

"Whoa! What happened? Oh, no. Not Trish," I said. I felt horrible. Trish was his youngest sister. She was five and was always smiling and playing.

Trey looked at me with tear-filled eyes. "I don't know what happened. I went out to the lines yesterday to check for rabbits and such. I got back in, and I know I closed the gate. I know it!" Trey raised his eyes to the sky and closed them tight. Fresh tears flowed and with a monumental effort got himself under control. He wiped his face and then started walking back to his house, and I followed. If there were four Trippers out here there might be more. I kept an arrow ready in my bow just in case.

We walked over to Trey's house, and it was just a mess over there. Trey's mom was holding her baby and crying; Trey's dad was holding his baby girl's hand and just shaking great big tears out. Trey's older sisters were just standing in the background with sad, shocked looks on their faces.

Trey put a hand on his dad's shoulder. "I got the Trippers, dad. Josh killed three, I got the last one."

Trey's dad looked over his shoulder at his son. A strange look came into his eyes as he stood up and faced his son. Trey's dad wasn't a big man, but at that moment he looked huge, wearing his grief like a second coat.

Trey's dad looked at me. "Thank you Josh. Trey, I'm going to ask you one question. Did you secure the gate yesterday?"

Trey looked up at his dad. "I did. Just like I always did, dad. I know I did!"

"Then how did the damn Trippers get in the yard to kill my baby?" Trey's dad roared at his son.

"Dad, I didn't!" Trey yelled.

"It wasn't his fault!" I said, probably louder than I should have.

Trey's dad focused his anger on me. "What do you know about it?" He took a step forward, and I took a step back, bringing up my bow.

"Stop!" I yelled. "I don't want to hurt you, Mr. Chambers! Trey didn't do it! I know he didn't!" I shouted as I stepped back to make room. Trey's family went silent as they watched me threaten to kill their father.

Trey's dad saw my bow and arrow ready to fly, and for a second he got angrier. But he must have seen in my eyes I was serious, and he backed off with his hands raised. "How do *you* know, Josh?" he asked with clenched teeth.

I told him about the man who propped open my gate last night and the arrow I put into him. I figured he must have done the same thing at Trey's house, but managed to do so without being caught. Unfortunately, Trish was outside when the Trippers came through.

When I finished my story, the change in Trey's dad and Trey was immediate. Both of them stared at me, and then Trey's dad brought his son in close for a deep hug. I heard him whisper he was sorry for yelling at him and hoped he could forgive him.

Trey's dad then came over to me. "I'm sorry, Josh. Please forgive me," he said in a small voice.

"I'm sorry for your loss," I said. "When you're ready, I can show you the blood trail and the footprints. I know which way he went."

Trey's dad nodded. "I have a daughter bury first. But I will be over soon."

I turned to leave, and Trey nodded his gratitude.

"Thanks, Josh. I owe you," Trey said.

"Let's just get this guy, huh?" I said.

CHAPTER 38

A day later in the morning, Mr. Chambers was out behind my house looking at the snow and the story it told. He swept back and forth, looking at the signs, and then started following a trail. He was armed with his hunting rifle, a handgun, and what looked like a baseball bat with big screws in it. Trey wasn't with him; he was staying behind to help back home. I personally thought Trey's dad was a little nuts for going off on his own, but then I realized he had survived the worst days of the infection and managed to keep his family alive, but things could happen. Hell, my own father died from Trippers, and he should have been one of the ones who lived.

After a while, Trey's dad was lost from view, and I started working on the chores that kept me busy. I let Judy run in the yard, and while she did that I walked the path down to the creek. The water was still flowing well, but there was a feeling of even colder weather coming, so I used my hatchet to break open a hole, and I gathered water in the two buckets I brought with. When I got back to the house, I filled Judy's water trough and then went up in the loft of the garage and took down a measure of hay. I filled Judy's feed bin, then got the shovel out for the worst of the chores. I swear that horse ate extra on purpose.

I got Judy back into the garage and gave her a rubdown to get the cold out of her. I didn't think I'd be taking her out anywhere today, so I buckled her blanket on her, and left her to her breakfast.

I checked the woodpile and brought up a few more hardwood logs to my room, and I worked the hand pump in the kitchen to clear the line and make sure it wasn't frozen. We had a freeze in the line a while back, and Dad cleared it out by pouring hot water back into the line and thawing it out.

I went down to the basement to check on my food stores, and I figured I had enough to last me the next two months. That would take me right about to the end of winter if I paced myself. I read in a book how to jerk meat and was trying it a corner of the basement. The rabbit strips I put up there were pretty stringy, but the venison jerky seemed to be doing well.

Once everything was done, I restarted the fire that had gone out, and soon the fireplace was a warm and inviting place. I stayed in the living room most of the time, usually because it was warmer. I had my books, I practiced my draw, and I worked on my education. My mother wouldn't want me to stop learning, so I worked my way through the textbooks she had and dove into the history books and literature. It took a me a few passes at Shakespeare before he started to make sense, but I really liked Poe and Steinbeck. Sometimes I felt like my mother was over my shoulder, smiling that I was still working at reading and educating myself.

On the day after Trey's dad had gone after the man who had opened the gates, Trey came over. He had to get out of the house as everything in there made him sad. I knew what he was going through and figured he just needed some friendship.

"Dad came back late last night," Trey said, gnawing on a piece of rabbit jerky.

"Did he catch the guy who opened your gate?" I asked.

Trey shook his head. "Nope. Dad got too far away from home following the trail and had to turn back. He couldn't stay away from his family."

"That's too bad." I said. "Maybe the guy will die from infection or blood loss from my arrow," I said.

Trey shook his head. "After the first couple miles Dad said he didn't see any blood trail anymore. He must have found a way to stop the bleeding."

"That sucks. Is he going out again?" I asked, washing down my jerky with some very cold water.

"Nope. He wants me to," Trey said.

I must have not done a good job of keeping the surprise off my face, because Trey pointed a finger at me.

"And you're coming, too," Trey said.

"We taking the horses?" I asked, thinking about what I would do with Judy if I was unable to bring her.

"Nope. To hear my dad talk about it, this guy was literally running a maze, trying to lose him. After a while, he lost the trail and came home. Judy will board with my family, and my older sister will stop by once a day to make sure everything is okay at your house. But we're moving out in an hour," Trey said. "I'll come get you, and we'll start again. With the snow we've had, we should get a good line on him, or at least a good idea where he's headed."

"All right, I'll get my cold weather gear and get ready." I stood up and looked at Trey. "And if we find him?" I asked.

"I kill him. I owe Trish that," Trey said.

I looked at him and saw the same look I had in my own eyes after my parents were killed. Trey had changed, too.

I changed my clothes and packed a backpack with supplies. I put my Colt in there along with a small pouch of spare ammo. I tied my quiver to the pack, and I made sure I had plenty of arrows. I kept my knife on my belt, and I packed spare socks, a spare shirt, and plenty of jerky. I also brought some cotton and matches. I put an extra blanket in there as well. It was a thin quilt made by my mom. Despite its light weight, it was very warm. I also brought my heater can, which my dad made for me, and a few small candles.

Trey came over, and together we secured the house, then we took Judy over to his barn. Pumpkin was happy to have company, and I could tell Judy was, too. Trey's family wished us luck, and Trey's dad had some words for us as we left.

"Don't take any chances. I'm sending you two because you're better trackers than I am, and you've had each other's backs since you were little. I'm forcing you to grow up a little faster than you should, but thanks to the damn virus, you haven't had much of a childhood anyway. You get this man, Trey. He's a danger to everyone who's trying to survive this mess. You get him, and don't think twice about it," he said.

Trey nodded, and we started walking up the road. Trey's dad told us he had followed the trail as it passed through subdivision. He marked the place where it had crossed the back road heading north, and we went that way.

In my own head, I wondered how much destruction this one man had caused, and what we might be walking into as we trailed him back to his lair.

CHAPTER 39

We didn't say much as we walked, and pretty soon we passed the Simpson's old house. The place was deserted, and there were still bones in the yard. The front door was open, and we could see where animals had been in and out.

Rounding the corner, we headed west and passed a few more homes. Some were occupied; some were not. As we moved I watched the sky, trying to figure out when the next snow was going to fall. If we were lucky, we would catch up to the man before the next heavy fall. If not, we'd lose him for good. I didn't see any snow on the horizon, and the sun was coming up, sending bright rays all through the world.

Up ahead, we saw a stick standing upright on the side of the road. A small string was tied around the top of the stick, holding another stick in place. The other stick was cut in two places, forming a small arrow that pointed north.

I cocked my head at the sign. "Geez. You'd think your dad had more confidence in us than that."

Trey shook his head. "This is tame compared to what he did when I was learning how to track. He once stuck a stick in every footstep a deer made just to make sure I saw the tracks."

"Well, let's see what we're after here," I said, bending down and taking a look at the tracks. I pushed the snow away from the imprint, being careful not to knock any on the print itself. The point here was to see if there were any strange things on the footprint that would distinguish it from others if it happened to cross another trail.

"Normal boot print," I said. "But look up here." I pointed to the toe of the boot which, based on instep, was the left foot. "There's a cut on the tread, third from the top. Looks like it's missing about half the tread."

Trey nodded. "All right. We got him. No place to run if he leaves a print anywhere. You ready?"

I brought my bow up and pulled my string from my inside pocket. That was a trick my dad taught me. If a bowstring was cold, it could snap, which could take your eye out if you were unlucky. I quickly strung my bow and gave it a test pull, keeping my face away from the string. Nothing snapped, so we were good for a while. If the temperature dropped, I was going to have to take the string off and warm it up.

"Let's do it. I'll watch the terrain; you keep your eye on the tracks," I said.

We walked into the yard of a home that had been abandoned and followed the tracks to the back yard. The home butted up against some railroad tracks, and we followed the trail down the train line for about a quarter mile west, then the tracks led north again, cutting through a hole in the thick brush.

Trey and I followed, and when the brush opened up, we found ourselves in another subdivision. The homes in this area were substantially larger than the ones we were used to.

"Looks like this area has been hit more than once, if you know what I mean," Trey said, following the tracks through the yard toward the main road.

"No kidding," I said. The houses, as big as they were, had been hit at least once by the Trippers and then again by looters and drifters. The one we passed had all of the ground floor windows busted in and a couple of the upstairs. It was too bad, since it seemed like it was a nice house.

The houses next to it were in the same condition, and all up and down the road the houses were the same way. Some had their garage doors open, and it looked like anything of use or value had been taken. One garage was huge, and my first thought was I could stable Judy in there with a friend and still have room for when Pumpkin came to visit.

My next thought when I looked at the homes was how hard it would be to heat one of those big places. Guess that wasn't a worry when everything worked back in the days before Tripp.

"Come on, the tracks lead this way," Trey said.

We followed the trail down across the road and into a small valley. As we walked, I could see a huge expanse of land spreading out to the east. It was loosely populated with trees, and a creek wound its way around the area. It would be the perfect place to run Judy if I could make sure it was safe.

A house was at the bottom of the valley, and it looked like it had once had people in it who had made it through the worst times. The yard was surrounded with a solid wood fence, and behind the house was a decent sized pond for water. I made a mental note to check this place out later when I had more time. Right now it looked shuttered and abandoned.

We followed the tracks to the creek as they swerved along the water, crossing a bridge. We moved across the entire open area, and on the other side was another subdivision. This one had homes that were even larger, and the tracks went right through the middle of them. I looked off to the east and saw the biggest home I had ever seen. It was at least four times the size of one of the homes we had passed, and was all pillars and windows.

"Jeez, who lived there?" I asked Trey, pointing at the big house.

Trey shook his head. "Dunno. Governor, maybe? Hey, watch yourself. The tracks go into that house."

"Got it. I'll check around back to see if he left," I said, circling around towards the rear of the house. I had to go through a garden gate, and I kept tripping over something hard in the snow. I circled wide and kept my arrow pointed at the house. If the man was there, he was going meet another pointy object in a hurry.

The back of the house was a tangled mess of trees and long grass. A large glass enclosure at the back of the house contained what looked like the remains of several large plants and even a couple of trees.

I checked the snow and found that the tracks led out the back door of the house and into the next yard. I whistled for Trey, and in a minute he was back leading the way.

CHAPTER 40

We walked past the houses and crossed what must have been another road. This one had more than a few tracks in it, and Trey and I slowed down. We didn't know if we were going to see drifters, Trippers, or what. We listened for a moment, then crossed the road, picking up the tracks on the other side.

I looked down the lane of houses, and for a brief moment wondered what it must have been like to live in this area when everything was normal.

I must have been daydreaming because I bumped into Trey. He was standing still next to a tree and staring straight ahead. He didn't even acknowledge the fact that I had bumped into him. He just stood very still.

I looked over his head and saw what had stopped him. In between the houses, right on the trail, was a large man. He was at least six feet four, if not larger, and his clothes were tattered beyond belief. His large hands were black with dirt and dried blood, and his face was dark as well, especially around the mouth. His eyes were deeply bloodshot which, according to what my dad had told me, indicated how long he had been infected. If they were light red, they had been infected for a few months to a year. If they were blood red, they had been infected for at least five years. This guy's eyes were a purple color which I took to mean he was probably an original. We were standing behind a small pine tree which had covered our approach. The blotches on the man's face were nearly black, giving him a very scary look.

The Tripper swayed from side to side, and he seemed like he was trying to make a decision. He put his hand out to touch the house, then he stumbled over to the other house to touch it as well. The journey was twenty yards across, but he only made a yard in our direction.

I pulled the arrow back until the fletching touched my cheek, then tracked him to the left. When it looked like he was going to stop for a second, I let the arrow go. The shaft flew straight past the man's head and into the side of the house.

It hit with a bang, and the Tripper's head snapped up. He had stumbled at the last second which had caused my arrow to miss. He looked at the arrow, then looked around. His hand reached out and touched the still quivering shaft that stuck out at an odd angle in the siding of the house. His eyes then scanned around, and his gaze fell on Trey and myself.

The Tripper's breath heaved out in an exaggerated wheeze, and he bared his teeth with the fury of a trapped animal. In a flash, he was stumbling backwards, the crossbow bolt that Trey had fired hit him squarely in the face, punching through his nose and spearing his brain. He flopped back into the snow, staring blankly at the brilliant blue sky that had witnessed millennia before this.

"Nice shot," I said, walking over to the house to try and get my arrow out. It had gone in between two boards, and with a little work I managed to get it out. The point was dented a bit, but I could fix that on a rock.

"Thanks." Trey walked over to the dead man and pulled his arrow out with a nasty squelch. He wiped it on the dead man's shirt and then rubbed some snow on it. He put it back in his cocked crossbow, and we continued on our way.

Right into a pack of Trippers. They saw us just as we saw them.

"Run!" Trey yelled, leaping forward.

I didn't need any more incentive than that. I used my dented arrow to put down the lead Tripper, and then I was right behind Trey. Trey stayed on the trail, only this time we were running instead of walking. It solved two problems. We were getting away from the infected and closing the gap on our gate crasher.

"Come on!" Trey said. He ran up to a house and bolted inside the open door. I was right behind him, and the wheezing, snarling Trippers were not far behind. Trey dodged and darted around furniture and debris, and finally got out the other side. He was halfway across the yard when I stopped him.

"Stay here, and make sure they see you," I said, returning to the house and closing the back door before moving through the snow towards the front of the house.

"What are you doing?" Trey said.

"You'll see," I said. I left Trey in the back yard and moved quickly towards the front of the house. When I reached the corner, I brought up my bow and used it to aim my eyesight as I slowly turned around to the front. Five Trippers were stumbling through the overgrown landscaping into the house, one right after the other. When the last one went in, I waited for a minute.

When I heard Trey shouting in the back yard, I ran towards the front door and closed it, slamming it shut. An instant after it closed, the door shook from an impact on the other side. I guess one of the Trippers happened to look back.

I ran to the back yard and met up with Trey again. I grinned at him, and I got a nodding smile in return.

"Not bad," Trey said. "If they don't break a window, we just might have saved a few people down the line."

"Let's get moving," I said. "We need to get to an area with a little more room to see. These houses are a trap."

"Well, the tracks lead that way, and we've got about five hours of daylight left," Trey said. "Maybe we need to move a little faster."

"Think you can keep to the track?" I asked, shifting my pack and making sure I could reach my arrows. The pack felt tighter than usual, but that was probably due to the fact that I was wearing more layers.

"We'll find out," Trey said. He verified that the track he was following was the one he wanted, and started after it. The trail led towards the east, then abruptly went through another hole in the brush heading north. We ducked through it and climbed up a small hill. At the top of the hill was a cleared path that ran out of sight both east and west. The path was flanked on both sides by heavy brush, and if there weren't any Trippers on this trail, one could travel in relative safety.

"Wonder what this used to be?" Trey said, looking back and forth.

"Not sure. But those look like mile markers, so people must have used it for some sort of travel," I said, pointing to a faded post with painted inscription of 3.4 mi. on it.

"Well, we'll take the horses on this sometime and let them have a nice long run on a level ground," Trey said.

"One of these days," I said. "Let's keep going."

The tracks led down the other side of the hill and towards what looked like another subdivision. As we moved, I was learning a little about our quarry. He was a shorter man with a measured stride. He didn't move like he was running anymore, and he probably figured he wasn't being followed. The trail didn't wander all over the place, and there was no attempt to hide the tracks. Either he didn't know we were coming, or he didn't care, a thought that made me pause a little, but when I spoke to Trey, he dismissed it out of hand.

"I doubt whatever he may have in mind for us that it figures on how fast you are with your gun," Trey said.

"My gun is in my pack." I said.

Trey looked at me. "Oh. Well, you're pretty quick with them arrows, aren't you?"

"Quick enough," I said.

"Hope it won't come to that," Trey said. "Hold it. Step back."

I moved into the shade of a tree that was close to the road. Trey ducked down and motioned with his hand that there was something ahead of us. I looked out on the other side of the tree and saw a Tripper stumbling up the road. He was moving away from us, and the speed at which he moved told me he was pursuing something, or something caught his eye and he wanted it.

"Can you get him?" Trey asked quietly.

I looked at the retreating Tripper. He was about forty yards off and moving pretty well. The snow slowed him down, but he was still plowing through pretty good. It would be a long shot, but I figured I could do it.

"Hang on," I said softly. "Is the scope broken on your crossbow?"

Trey actually had the grace to look embarrassed. "Jesus. I forgot," he said. He brought up his own weapon, sighted the Tripper, and released the bolt. The arrow was a black streak across my vision, and then the Tripper was falling down, having had his skull penetrated by a rather rude arrowhead.

"Nice shot," I said. I was truthful when I said it. It was a good shot.

"Thanks. Come on," Trey said. "You hear that?"

I listened for a minute. "Sounds like a fight," I said. It did, too. There was a lot of snarling, banging, and some odd sounding thumps that I hadn't heard before.

CHAPTER 41

"Let's go see." Trey said. He paused long enough to reload his crossbow, and we both went up the long hill, passing house after house on an odd stretch of road. It was odd because it went nowhere. It literally ran smack up into the trees that closed off the other subdivision. The contrast between the homes couldn't be more different. These homes were small, with maybe twenty to thirty feet on a side. The other homes were easily sixty to eighty feet on a side.

At the top of the hill we could see a little better. There was yet another subdivision in front of us, and from our small vantage point, we could see that it was a vast network of roads and houses.

"Damn, that's a lot of houses," I said.

"Damn, that's a lot of Trippers," Trey said.

I looked in the direction he was and nearly dropped my bow. Near what looked like another main road was a strange building that was mostly glass in the front. But the stranger thing was a young woman standing on top of a metal bin swinging a club at several Trippers who were crowding around and snarling and grabbing at her legs. When one would get close, she would smack it with the club and knock it away, but she couldn't get close enough to really kill one or two, because the other ones would pull her down. The wall behind her was too tall for her to climb, so she really had nowhere to go. A small pack was in the snow about fifty feet away from the dumpster, and it was easy to see that she had been surprised by this group, and had retreated to the only place of marginal safety.

"I've got enough arrows," I said. "Let's get to a spot where they can't see where the shafts are coming from."

We ran over to a couple of trees that were close to the road, and I saw the woman watch us run. She was experienced enough to stamp her feet and keep the attention of the Trippers on her, so we were able to get into position without being chased there. If I had more time to argue about it, I might have lobbied for a higher position in the house across the street.

I took the right side and aimed for the nearest ones in the back of the crowd. They were about sixty feet away, so it wasn't that difficult of a shot. I hit the first one in the back of the head, and she dropped like she had been struck with a sledgehammer. Trey fired while I was drawing another arrow, and he put down a short older man. I fired again, killing another Tripper. They hadn't figured out where we were or even that their friends were dying.

Trey's next shot went wild, since his target ducked her head for a moment. It glanced off her skull, careened upward and struck the wall behind the woman mere inches from her head.

"Hey!" she yelled, ducking with her hands up.

For whatever reason, probably because he was raised to be polite, Trey held up a hand and yelled out.

"Sorry!"

Every Tripper in that pack turned our way. They caught sight of us since we weren't that well hidden by the trees and started our way.

"Are you kidding me?" I asked out loud, firing an arrow at the nearest Tripper. He went down without a fuss, and I put another one down quickly. It was easier to hit them since they were getting closer. I put two down to every one Trey put down, and we made short work of that pack.

I had to wonder a little bit about how we had grown in the last couple of months. Just last fall we would have run like hell from these Trippers. Of course, last fall we didn't have any of our family members killed, so there was that.

When the last of the infected fell, Trey and I went around and collected our arrows and bolts, wiping them off carefully on the dead clothing, running them through the snow, and wiping them off again. While we were doing this, the woman who had taken refuge on the container had gotten down, and she picked up her pack on her way over to us.

She as about twenty or so and a little taller than me. Her hair was pulled back in a ponytail, held in place by a small leather band. Her coat was a little bigger than it needed to be, which told me she was wearing a man's coat. She reminded me of my mom when my mother used to put on my dad's coat to run outside in the fall to scare away the crows from the garden.

"Thanks you two. I thought I was going to die by Tripper or from the cold," she said. "What are you guys doing out here all by yourselves?" She had a straight talking way about her that made you want to tell the truth, and judging by the fact she was travelling by herself meant she was capable of handling herself in most situations.

"Hunting a man," Trey said. He reloaded his crossbow and slung it over his shoulder. "You seen anyone headed north, maybe looking like he was wounded?"

The woman nodded. "I passed up a guy like that about three hours ago. He was holding his side and muttering something about being trapped, and he was going to let them all out." She looked at us. "I'm Kim, by the way," she said, holding out her hand. She kept her other hand under her coat, and I didn't trust that.

"Josh," I said. I kept my bow in between us as I shook her hand. I met her eye, and she nodded slightly.

My friend shook her hand next. "Trey. Nice to meet you. We need to get moving," Trey said that last towards me. He started towards the road and then started a slow circle, looking for the tracks.

Kim watched him for a minute, then she turned to me. "Where do you live?" she asked casually.

I wasn't so young that I trusted everyone I met. My dad had pounded that instinct into me since I could walk. He had seen the worst of human nature even before the end of civilization and knew that trust was something to be earned.

"South of here," I said. I watched Trey but kept an eye on Kim.

"Any more homes that way?" Kim asked.

I shrugged. "Down this road and through the hole in the brush will bring you to a subdivision with a bunch of huge homes. Take your pick," I said.

"Really?" Kim asked. "Thanks." She started walking but then stopped.

"How far north are you going?" Kim asked.

"Until we get our man," I said. "Hopefully we can catch up before nightfall. Why?"

"Things get bad as you go north, and the further you go, the worse it gets." Kim started walking again. "Just a friendly warning."

"Thanks," I said. I started walking towards Trey who was waving for me to catch up. I stopped and called back to her.

"Hey Kim!"

"What?"

"Stay out of the white house with the pines trees in the back yard," I yelled. "We trapped about seven Trippers in there, so they might not be friendly."

"Thanks!"

CHAPTER 42

I caught up to Trey, and he gave me a look before he started up a road.

"You and your girlfriend have a good chat?" Trey asked.

"Don't be a jerk," I said, irritated by his tone.

"Just don't want you to forget your mission here," Trey replied.

"I lost my family to Trippers, too," I said. "And this guy opened *my* gate first."

Trey stopped and looked at me hard. "You saying you got dibs?"

I returned his look. "I'm saying I'm here to help you, but you ain't the only one who's suffered in this world."

Trey looked at me for a long time, and for a moment I thought he was going to take a swing at me. I was ready for it, and shifted my feet ever so slightly. Trey must have remembered that we were here for the same reason, and he visibly relaxed.

"Sorry, man. I just want this over with," Trey said quietly, returning to the trail.

"No problem. I loved your little sister, too," I said. I did, too. She always had a smile for me and treated me like I was just another big brother to play with. I wanted revenge for her nearly as much as Trey.

We followed the trail into the subdivision, and I kept an eye on the sun. It was well into the afternoon, and we were going to have to find a place to spend the night.

The homes in this area were much smaller than the ones we had seen on the other side of the trail. They were much smaller than my own home and Trey's. They were packed pretty closely together, and as we walked I could see that this area had been hit pretty hard. Home after home looked like it had been broken into, and in some places we could see black marks of old blood, and in a few homes we could see the remains of some of the former occupants as they lay upon the floors and stairs. A lot of the bones we saw were broken.

The trail led right up the street, never straying from a straight line. He was headed north, and as we stayed on the path I kept thinking about what Kim had said. If things were going to get worse the further north, we got then we were sending ourselves into the teeth of trouble. I wondered if I should get my gun out of my pack when Trey pointed ahead.

"Is that a person?" Trey asked.

I squinted to try and see over the glare of the sun on the snow. There seemed to be a person walking ahead of us, but he was moving slow and weaving slightly from side to side. His walk was like that of a Tripper, but after years of watching these things, you got a sense as to how they moved and were able to tell one at a distance. This one was pretty close to walking like a Tripper, but he straightened out too many times to fully convince me.

"Not sure," I said. "One way to find out." I figured he was about a hundred yards ahead of us, and it was going to stretch the limit of my bow, but I was willing to lose an arrow at this point.

I pulled the string back to my cheek and raised the arrow up to nearly a forty-five-degree angle. "Be ready. If it's a Tripper, he'll stop at the arrow. If it's our guy, he'll probably run."

"Let 'er rip," said Trey, unslinging his crossbow.

I fired the arrow, and it sailed up into the air. I watched its flight and tried to figure out where it was going to land. The wind gave it a push to the right, and it streaked for the ground. The shaft landed upright in the snow about ten feet in front of the walker. If he had been a little faster, the arrow would have hit him in the head, and it would have been the most amazing shot I had ever tried up to that moment.

The person ahead of us stopped and looked at the arrow. He turned around and looked back at us, and even at that distance I could feel his scrutiny. He turned away from us and started away, walking a little faster than he had been before.

"That's alive. He's our guy!" Trey pointed to the footprints that led to the man, and they were the same as the ones we had been following. "Come on!"

Trey started to run, and I had no choice but to keep up. I pulled an arrow out of my quiver and in my haste to nock it I dropped in the snow. As I bent down to pick it up, I got a very good look at the tracks we had been following. The left foot was fine, no problem there. But as I took a long, good look at the right foot, I saw a dark stain on the outside of the print. I looked at the next couple of prints and a few of the ones behind us and I saw the same thing.

Years of tracking animals in the woods led to one unmistakable conclusion: the man we were chasing was bleeding, and had been for a long time. How he was still able to keep going was a mystery.

"Josh! Move your ass!" Trey yelled at me.

"Right behind you!" I said. I didn't have time to talk about what I had seen, although I had a sneaking suspicion Trey already knew what was in those tracks.

We ran towards our quarry, and as we approached, the man began to stumble more. The exertion was wearing him out, and he was having a hard time staying on his feet. Still, he kept up the chase, and we were deep into another subdivision when he finally fell down.

Trey and I spread out and both of us had our arrows aimed at him. He was lying on his side in the snow, and his breathing was shallow and labored. As we got closer, I could see he was a man about my dad's age, wearing all black clothing. His hair was matted and damp, and his face was flushed, like he had been running for a lot longer than we had seen.

"Hey! Hey you!" Trey yelled. He got close to the man and pushed him over on his back. The man rolled, and his eyes opened. He looked around and then closed his eyes again.

I looked at him and saw there was a darker stain down on his side. Using the tip of my bow, I pulled his jacket away and saw the wound from one of my arrows bleeding from under his rib cage. I guess I had hit him harder than I thought.

"Guess you won't be opening any more gates, huh? Guess you won't be letting any more little girls die, huh?" Trey was in the man's face, shouting and crying at the same time.

"Trey. Trey!" I yelled. I pulled him up and pushed him away. "He's done! Leave him be."

Trey raised his crossbow and was about to shoot at the man when I stepped in front of him.

"He's done, Trey. He's finished." I pointed at the man on the ground. "I killed him when I put that arrow in him."

Trey's eyes cleared, and he took a good look at the man on the ground.

"Yeah, you're right." Trey looked away. "I saw the blood on his trail when we crossed into this area. I figured we would have run him to ground before now."

"Nice of you to tell me," I said.

"Let them out."

Trey looked at me. "What did you say?"

"I didn't say anything," I said.

We both looked down at the man on the ground.

His head moved back and forth, and his eyes glazed over as they stared up at the sky. He blinked slowly and spoke again, softly.

"Let them out. Open the gates. Let them out. Lights. So many lights," he whispered

Trey snorted. "Dude's delirious. He's thinking about all the gates he's opened and people he's killed."

"Open the gates. Lights. So many lights."

I shook my head. "What lights?" I wondered.

"Not our problem. We gonna finish him?" Trey asked.

I looked down. "Not really. He'll be dead soon anyway, and we owe him for Trish. At least we know he's finished killing anyone else," I said.

Trey nodded. "I want to see him dead. I have to tell my dad I saw him dead."

The man below us whispered a few more things in his delirium, and after about twenty more minutes, passed away. His last breath was a long exhale, and we waited for a few more minutes before we were sure. Even so, Trey took out his knife and stabbed the man in the throat. If he had any life left in him, it was gone now. I didn't try to stop Trey. He needed that for his sister.

"Well, that's that," Trey said, wiping off his knife. He looked at the sky. "We ain't going to see home before dark; we'd better get to some place safe."

"Well, let's pick a place and set up for the night," Trey said.

He started walking off to the north, and I fell in behind. I couldn't help but think about what the man had said. I had a gut feeling he wasn't talking about fence gates, but something else. And what was he talking about lights? That made no sense at all.

We were all alone out here, and there hadn't been lights for years. That just didn't make any sense.

CHAPTER 43

"Do you think they saw us?"

"I have no idea. We'll know soon enough."

"Where did they all come from?"

"Just were there. We were in the middle of a big bunch of houses."

"How many arrows do you have left?"

I ran a hand over my quiver. "Twelve," I said. "Don't have the time to make more, and I doubt there's any archery stores around here."

Trey looked at his pack. "I have four. Dammit!"

"Shh!" I said. I raised my head up slightly to try and see if the Trippers that had chased us here had heard us. I looked out the window quickly and reported back to Trey.

"They're still out there, but they aren't leaving the house we ran through," I said.

Trey and I had chased a man for about five miles through three subdivisions full of homes. The man had opened my gate, and had opened Trey's. I managed to catch the man in the act and had put an arrow in him, which eventually had killed him. But not before Trey's little sister had been killed by Trippers who had gotten into their yard. We followed a blood trail and saw it through to the end, but we didn't get out fast enough, and had found our way back cut off by a large group of infected.

They had chased us another mile north, and we finally slowed them down by shooting several of them, but they got reinforcements that renewed the pursuit and we were forced to run again. Night was coming fast, and if we stayed where we were, we were going to be killed. Trippers came out in force at night; no one ever really knew why. Maybe the darkness felt better on their eyes, who knew? But an unsecured house was a death trap, and we both knew people who had died when a Tripper horde descended upon the unwary.

"You ready?" Trey asked.

"Now or never," I said. I hefted the plates I had taken from the kitchen of the house we were hiding in and readied one in my hand.

"Go!" Trey said, running out the back door. He had two plates of his own, and as we left, he through them through the left window by the door. I threw mine through the right windows, and we slipped through the narrow opening between the houses on the other side of the backyards. We cut north again, and ran like there was no tomorrow. If we got caught, there wouldn't be.

The breaking glass and plates caused a bit of an uproar, and we could hear the angry growls and wheezes as the Tripper horde descended on the house we had just evacuated. They would spend a few minutes poking around the place, but hopefully that would buy us just enough of a window to get the hell out of there.

Trey ran north, as our path to the south and home was blocked. The plan might have been to go north, then east, then cut back south to get home, but for right now I wasn't thinking that far ahead. Dad always said you need to think of the immediate future that was going to happen, not the future you wished would happen.

"Come on, this way!" Trey said. He ran up a long road that had a lot of large houses on one side of the street, and smaller homes on the other. The strange thing was every house facing the road had a fence blocking the yard. But for us, it was a free passageway that promised not to have any Trippers on it.

"Hang on," I said, stopping to catch my breath. We had been running flat out for about ten minutes, and I was getting out of breath. The air was still very cold, and trying to breathe it took almost as much energy as running.

I had stopped near a brick building that was near the side of the road. A playground with its plastic slides and swings looked like it was as ready for as good a time now as it had been in the past. In the distance, a large brick building stood in an open area surrounded by houses.

"Wonder what that was for," I said, sipping on a little water from my canteen.

"Housing Trippers," Trey said, shielding his eyes against the setting sun to look over the building. "There's about forty coming out of the building now. Looks like they might have heard our little distraction."

"Moving on," I said. I put away my canteen and followed Trey.

We were two small targets running against the dying light, hoping we could find some shelter to keep us alive for another day. If Trippers got in front of us, we'd have to take our chances in another house, but as we knew, hiding from the infected rarely worked. It was like they instinctively knew where you were hiding.

A crossroads greeted us when we ran out of buildings, and Trey and I stood there for a moment trying to figure out what to do.

"North?" Trey asked.

I shook my head. "Kim said North got worse the farther we travelled. We'd better go East," I said. "If we head east for a bit, find a place to stay, we could head south, get around these Trippers, and get home."

"Closest thing I've heard to a plan all day."

Trey started out at a slow jog, and I followed. We used this jog before when we were running down a deer. After a while, the deer would just give up because it couldn't run anymore.

We ran east, passing several tall buildings. They looked like single story houses stacked on top of each other with all the garages on the first floor. I'd never seen anything like it, and it was fascinating to look at while we ran.

The road opened up, and to the north I could see a huge road. There were six lanes, and it stretched my imagination to try and see all the cars that could fill that highway. I knew those roads once led to the rest of the country, but the wall stopped them at the state line.

"Hey, what's that?" Trey asked.

I looked at what he was pointing at, and it appeared to be a huge building of some kind. The walls were a faded red, and next to it was another huge building. It went on for a while, and behind it was another building. This one was a square with a large blue front that stuck up at an angle. It didn't serve any purpose I could think of.

"Looks like it might have been one of those shopping centers Mom talked about. Lots of stores and things to buy," I said, stepping around a large branch that had fallen on the road.

"Worth checking out?" Trey asked.

"Doubt there's anything left, and we need to find a place for the night," I said. "We have an hour at most before we're up to our necks in Trippers."

Most of the time Trippers stayed indoors or under some sort of cover during the day. It took some strange event to rouse them to wander on their own. At night, however, they came out in force, and that was when anyone not infected had better find a place to hide or get behind some sturdy walls.

"Well, let's follow the road that's in front of it, and we can check it out from there," Trey said.

I could tell Trey really wanted to look into the stores, and I couldn't blame him. The only way we got anything new in this world was to either make it, find it, or trade for it. I had hit the jackpot with my Colt, although it cost me my father. If I could trade it back for him, I'd do it in a heartbeat.

"We can look, but we really need to get to some shelter," I said.

Trey led us down the road, and at the next intersection he turned north. This took us up a small hill, and we found ourselves looking out over a long stretch of that big road I saw earlier.

"There's something you could use," Trey said, pointing across the way.

"Doubt there's anything left in there, but I wouldn't mind a look," I said. Trey had pointed to a sporting goods store, and I would have liked to see if there were any arrows in there. I could make my own, and I had a lot back home; neither situation helped me right now.

"Nice view up here," Trey said.

"It was," I replied, pointing south. I whipped an arrow out of my quiver and nocked it, bringing the string back to my cheek. I barely aimed before I let it go, sending it into the head of the Tripper who came out of the ditch.

It was a decent shot, but it was a wasted effort, since five more came out of the ditch as well.

"Jesus! Run!" Trey yelled.

CHAPTER 44

I didn't need to be told twice. I kept pace with Trey as the pack of Trippers wheezed and roared behind us. They couldn't run as fast as we could, but then they didn't need to rest, either. Eventually they would run us down like Trey and I used to do to the deer. I would have thought about the irony if I wasn't worried about dying.

We ran over the hill and down the street. At the next intersection, we turned west and as we did, I happened to look over to my right.

"Trey! This way!" I said, working my way through some thick snow between a couple of small buildings. I saw a building that held the promise of safety if we could just get to it.

"What did you see?" Trey asked, stepping in my tracks to get through the snow faster.

"You'll see." I hoped the two buildings would mask our escape, and the Trippers would lose our trail.

We passed another building, a large office type. It was about four stories and was covered in glass windows with a simple front. The doors had been smashed open, and we could see that there once had been violence in there. It looked a little like what a hospital would have looked like given what my dad had told me.

"Come on, it's right back here!" I said, running at an angle away from the building. I was trying to make sure we stayed out of sight of the Trippers.

Trey saw the building I was heading to. "Now that might work. If we block the stairwell, we're good to go."

The building was six stories tall and designed in a cylindrical fashion. What made this building unique was the fact that there wasn't a ground floor. There was just a small section that had a stairwell leading up to the second floor and beyond.

We ran to the stairwell, and we just able to squeeze past a broken door and desk that had been tossed down the stairs. If we had been bigger, we never would have been able to get through.

Trey and I pushed the desk until it blocked the doorway completely, then angled the door to hold the outer door in place. We got out of that stairwell since the whole thing was glass, and we could be seen if we didn't move.

At the top of the stairs was a reception area and what looked like some offices. I went into a room that was nearby and over to the window. I wanted to see if the Trippers had seen us. If they had, we had to get out the way we came in. If not, we could spend the night here relatively safely, since it was doubtful the Trippers could open the door.

The room I was in had a bed, a dresser, and a small bathroom. The window on the far end of the room was covered in curtains, and I opened one slightly to look out. I could see the road and the small buildings we passed. I could see the Trippers as well as they moved on down the road, having lost our trail.

I could also see the bars on the window that were secured to the outside of the building.

"Wonder what these are for?" I asked, pointing out the bars to Trey.

Trey shrugged. "Can't imagine what they were meant to keep out."

"Or in," I said.

"That too."

"Should we see if we are alone?" I asked.

"Honestly? I'd rather just stay here and hunker down for the night," Trey said.

I shook my head. "Your dad and my dad taught us better than that."

"I really hate it when you're right," Trey sighed.

I unstrung my bow and let it rest, taking the string and looping it into a pocket on my coat. It would be useless in close quarters anyway. I took off my pack and took my Colt out, sliding the holster onto my belt. I didn't have my other gun belt, so this would have to do. Trey moved his crossbow to the front since it took up less space than my recurve, and he could use it in tighter quarters than I could.

"So this building makes a complete circle," I said. "We should be able to check the rooms on this floor pretty quickly, and we can leave our stuff here."

"Works for me. You take the left side; I'll take the right," Trey said.

We walked steadily forward, looking into rooms and seeing if there were any surprises for us. It was very creepy since it was getting dark, and the shadows were playing tricks with our eyes. Most of the rooms were identical, just a bed, a bathroom, and a window. Some had dressers, some didn't. None of them had anyone in them, so we were feeling pretty good about our hiding place. I looked again out the window and didn't see any Trippers come our way, so that was another good sign.

The second and third floors were the same as the first, only it was getting harder to see. We couldn't turn a light on, because that would have been like a beacon to the Trippers. For whatever reason, they could see pretty well in the dark.

The fourth floor was unoccupied as well, but instead of having beds, the rooms were empty. There were no bathrooms, and the doors to the rooms were heavier, with little windows on them. The windows in the rooms were dark, with no curtains. It almost looked like the windows had been painted over.

"Wonder what happened up here," Trey whispered.

"Not sure," I said. "I wouldn't want to spend any time in those rooms. Give me open sky any day."

The fifth floor was the same—unoccupied, but still creepy. The sixth floor, though, was the one that really didn't look like anything that was good for anyone.

At the top of the stairs to the sixth floor, we had to push through a heavy steel door. Once past that, we found ourselves in a familiar hallway, but the layout was different. Instead of several rooms, the walls were taken out of the rooms so each room was the size of four of the ones on the other floors. Each room was slightly different, but all of them had a very sinister feel about them.

The air itself was oppressive and thick, and I kept looking over my shoulder, expecting to see whatever it was that was staring holes into the back of my head. Every time I looked, however, there was nothing there.

"What the hell was this place?" Trey asked. He walked over to the bed that was positioned in the middle of the floor. The sheets were torn and dirty, and there looked to be some kind of stain running down the side of the bed. But the thing that had drawn Trey's attention was the leg restraints and the handcuffs attached to the bed.

"No idea," I said. I kept getting that feeling, but I didn't bother looking back anymore. I had an idea who or what it was that was staring at me.

"Hate to think what we might have found on the seventh or eighth floors if this place had them," Trey whispered.

"Probably a dungeon," I whispered back.

We both snickered at that, and it helped release some of the tension that was nearly visible in the room. We went back into the hallway and kept going.

I was scared, I'm not ashamed to admit, and as the sun slipped away, the darkness in the building was nearly crushing. But we kept on, finding room after room with those strange beds in them. At the end of the circle, right before the stairs, Trey stopped to pick up a piece of paper on the floor.

It was a memo of some kind, and the writing was nearly illegible. But at the top of the paper I could read the words "Tinley Park Mental Health Center."

"Did we just take refuge in a former insane asylum?" I asked.

"I won't tell if you won't," Trey said seriously.

"Deal."

"My dad would whip both of us," Trey said.

I believed it, and we would have earned it, too.

"Well, it's empty, anyway, so let' get back to our stuff and hunker down for the night. The first floors seemed like the most harmless," I said.

"Deal."

CHAPTER 45

We went back to our packs and found a room to stay in. I dragged a mattress from another room into this one, and we spread out for the night. Trey found some wool blankets in a closet, so we were set. We locked the door after checking we could get it open from the inside, and made sure the drapes were secured. Trey wanted to start a fire in the metal waste can, but I pointed out that the glow from that would be hard to miss in the dark, even through the curtains.

"How about a candle?" Trey said. "Anything to push back the gloom in this place."

"That should be okay," I said. I fished around and pulled out a small flat candle. It was about an inch tall and about inch in diameter. They weren't good for more than a little light or heating up a small can of water. I put it in my little lantern which was nothing more than an old soda can with a square cut out of the front. The hole in the top let the smoke and heat out, while the aluminum interior helped reflect more light than was possible otherwise. It wouldn't keep us warm, but it was better than the darkness. Hopefully by the time the candle went out we would be asleep.

Trey took the mattress off the bed, and we arranged the beds so we would be sleeping head to head. It would allow us to talk without being heard by anyone who wasn't within two feet of us. I lit the candle and pointed it away from the window, the warm glow of the light driving away the shadows and giving the impression of a small fire.

I hadn't realized how exhausted I was until I lay down, and suddenly I could barely move my head. I closed my hood over my face, and when I said good night to Trey, I didn't get an answer. I guess he was even more tired than I was. I was looking forward to getting home tomorrow. I had had enough of chases and winter.

My last thought before I drifted off completely was wondering if Kim had found shelter for herself. Guess I'd never know.

In the morning, Trey and I carefully went out of the building. The sun was bright on the snow, and it was hard to see very clearly. One thing that stood out was the large number of footprints that were around the building and the entrance. There had to have been thirty to forty footprints around the grounds. No one was in sight this morning, thankfully.

When I saw those prints, a very cold chill that had nothing to do with the outside air ran up my spine. I could see Trey felt the same way since he was unusually quiet as he looked at the prints. I knew what he was thinking, since I was thinking the same thing. We'd be dead right now if those Trippers had figured out how to get in the building.

As turned out, Trey wasn't thinking about that at all.

"The tracks of this crowd go south, same way we need to go. We need to get around them somehow," Trey said.

"I've never seen a map of this area," I said. "When my father and I rode out that one time, we went east, not north."

Trey shook his head. "My dad has a map of this area, but I haven't looked at it for a long time. I feel like there's some water that way." Trey pointed to the northeast.

"That might be the way to go," I said. "If we can get to the water, we can follow it east to the wall. Take the wall south, and we can get home the same way my father and I did that one time."

"Well, we need to do something," Trey said. "Let's get moving."

"How about we start off in the right direction?" I suggested. "That road right there leads east, and we can head north when we come to another road."

"Sounds like the best plan so far. You can lead," Trey said.

I shrugged, not really caring about who led the way. I walked across a grassy area and found the road on the other side of what looked like a deep ditch. I jumped the ditch easily, but Trey needed a hand since his legs weren't as long as mine.

Following the road we wanted, we passed a huge building on the right. The faded sign said hotel and convention center. I knew what a hotel was, but a convention center was a new one for me. Whatever it was, there was a huge hole in the center of the roof. The blackened edges of the hole suggested a fire at some time in the past, and the broken windows of the hotel told me that place was not friendly to our cause.

I turned north at the first major road I could find, and it was a long road that led through a small town. The town was centered around a train station, and there were the remnants of shops and restaurants down this street. Trey was fascinated with the railroad tracks, looking at them disappear over the horizon.

"How far do you think they go?" Trey asked.

"You know how far," I said. "Mom gave us a lesson on the railroads that crossed the country once upon a time. I'd bet we could take that track all the way to Mexico if we could get over the wall."

Trey nodded. "Be nice to go anywhere," he said quietly.

"You can," I said. "You can cross the wall, deal with Trippers every day for the rest of your life."

Trey snorted. "No thanks. I'll take the ones we have."

We moved quickly, and along the way a small building caught my eye. It was a business, but it looked like a house. The sign above the door read Sporting Goods, which piqued my interest.

"Detour?" I asked.

Trey looked at the building. "Why not?"

We stepped over to the building, and I tried the door. It came open easily enough, and then fell off the rusty hinges to land at my feet. I danced back and nearly fell down as the door tripped me up.

"Graceful," Trey said. He walked up to the entrance and looked in. "Well, this looks interesting."

I gathered myself and followed Trey inside. The interior of the building was crowded with outdoor sports gear. There was camping gear, hiking gear, and hunting gear. We'd stumbled upon a treasure trove of supplies and survival gear. In one section of the small store I found the archery section, and I nearly danced when I found a box full of arrows. Searching the nearby shelves yielded a box of field points, and a box of broad head tips.

Trey was looking at a large knife when I presented him with a handful of crossbow bolts complete with razor tipped shafts. He dropped the knife and took the bolts.

"Damn! Thanks, man!" he said as he put them in his quiver. "Did you find some for…yes, you did." Trey smiled as he saw my full quiver.

I looked at the shelf behind the counter where Trey was standing and saw there were some boxes of ammunition that had been pushed out of sight. I went around the counter's edge and walked past some strange racks. They were a mystery until I realized they used to hold guns, probably rifles.

I pulled the ammo forward and saw that they were a box of 9mm cartridges, and two little boxes of .22 ammunition. I put the ammo in my pack since I had guns that could use the bullets.

"Hey Josh! Come look at this," Trey called to me from the other side of the store. He was over at the archery section and was pulling something down from a hook on the side of a tall section of shelves.

It was a bow, but unlike any I had ever seen. It was compact with three strings connecting some wheels that were on the end of the limbs. The riser was much smaller than my bow's, and there was a funny looking ring with small points sticking out the side of it. Holding the bow and looking through it like I was going to use it, I saw the little points lined up like the sights on my gun, and realized it was used for aiming.

"I'll be," I said. "I wonder what the draw weight is?"

"Give it a pull," Trey said.

I pulled back on the center string, and the pull was very hard. It came back about six inches, and suddenly I was surprised by the let up as the string came all the way back.

"That was weird," I said, releasing the string slowly. I expected it to go slow and then snap forward, but it was smooth all the way.

Trey picked up the manual that was still hanging on the hook and read the first few lines. "Mission Craze compound bow. Adjustable draw weight from 15 to 70 pounds. Huh. Must be those crazy wheels on the thing." Trey picked up an arrow. "Give it a try."

"What the hell," I said. "Do we need anything else from here?" I asked.

"Not that we can carry. I grabbed some candles and matches, but we really need to bring the horses back here and clean up. This place has too much to leave behind." Trey said.

"Let's get the door back up," I said. "Then I'll try the bow."

We wrestled the door back up into the frame, and made it look like the store had never been visited. Trey stood on a handrail and took down the sign that identified this place as a sporting goods store. We were going to keep this treasure to ourselves. If we played our cards right, we could empty this place and set up our own little shop somewhere, and make a profit off of this.

As we stepped down the stairs, Trey slapped me on the arm. A Tripper was headed our way, coming down the street from the north. The tree-lined street was a patchwork of sun and shade, and the Tripper went from shade to shade, trying to reach us as it walked along.

"Guess I can try the bow out now," I said. I nocked the arrow and pulled the string back to my cheek. The sights were a little weird to me, but I remembered what my dad said about sights, and lined them up on the Tripper. He was about fifty yards away and closing fast. I held the string back for a second, and in that second I realized that holding this string was a lot easier than on my old bow.

I released the arrow and it streaked towards the Tripper. I didn't even see it's flight and suddenly the Tripper was down.

"Holy cow," Trey said.

I looked at the compound bow with new respect. That arrow had taken off in a hurry and had never slowed down.

We walked cautiously over to the Tripper, and I saw the arrow had hit him in the center of his face. All that was sticking out of the front of his head was the fletching. The point had punched out the back of his skull, and there was about eighteen inches of arrow shaft sticking out of the back of his head.

"Damn," I said. I looked at the bow and realized it was set to forty pounds, which was fifteen pounds heavier than my recurve. I wondered what this bow could do at the seventy-pound setting?

"Did you aim for his head?" Trey asked, watching the snow around the man's skull turn red and black.

"I did, actually," I said.

"Damn. Nice bow," Trey said.

"You want it?" I asked. "I have my other one."

Trey shook his head. "You've always been better than me with a bow. If it weren't for the scope on my crossbow, I'd miss the ground."

"All right then." I took off my pack and secured the new bow to the back. Even though it shot flatter and harder than my old one, I was so used to my old bow and knew how to shoot it that I'd have to spend weeks practicing with the new one to come close to the same efficiency.

I packed the instruction manual as well; no point in losing an eye when trying to change the limb strength.

CHAPTER 46

We moved north, passing dozens of old stores and buildings. The tree-lined street was quiet, and the snow on the ground gave us good warning of any activity in the area. We saw several large groups of footprints, and on a couple of occasions we saw smaller numbers. The Trippers were easy to identify. All we had to do was look for the bare feet. The people who might be alive wore boots, and sometimes there were tracks of wagons, sleds, and the odd dog.

"Did you notice all of the tracks we've seen, they were all headed south?" Trey asked.

"And we're headed north," I replied.

"Are we the stupid ones?"

"Maybe there will be no one left by the time we get there," I said hopefully.

Trey didn't bother to answer that one.

We stayed close to trees and the edges of the roads, making ourselves as invisible as possible. Trippers could see well enough, but daylight seemed to hurt their eyes. Never could tell with them, though.

We crossed a major road, and to the west I could see large buildings. They were enormous and seemed to go on for a long time. We saw several tall buildings reaching up ten or more stories. I wondered what we could see if we went up there.

The buildings thinned out, and the road thinned as well. The trees were reaching over the road creating a kind of tunnel that blocked out light. Trey and I moved through it quickly, as neither of us much cared for things like that.

On our left was a subdivision of long houses. They were two stories tall, but they looked like three houses put together. It was an odd thing to see, but what made it more odd was every door on every house was open.

"Wonder why those doors are like that?" I asked.

"Maybe looters wanted to know which houses they had already been to," Trey said.

"I don't know; it seems really weird to me. Something's not right," I said.

"What's the matter?" Trey asked.

"Well, there's just something wrong. Oh, hell."

"Run!"

"I don't know where we're going!"

"Just *run!*"

I took off to the north, following the road we had been on. There looked to be a large forest ahead of us, and if we could make it, it would slow down the Trippers that had poured out of the buildings like a diseased avalanche. Several of them were pretty fast walkers, and we were hard pressed to keep ahead of them. Our legs weren't as long, and we could hear them wheezing as they got closer and closer.

"We ain't gonna make it, Josh!" Trey yelled, trying to keep up. We ran around a corner and followed another road north. The woods to our left were sparse and would hardly have slowed this crowd down. A quick look behind me showed at least a hundred if not more of the damned things.

"Hang on! Just keep going!" I was panting now, trying to stay ahead of the Trippers who had outpaced their kin, and were closing fast. I drew the string back on my bow, and suddenly stopped and turned, swinging my weapon around. The Tripper was a lot closer than I thought, and I could see his splotched face with his bloodshot eyes barreling down on me.

I didn't even aim, I just let the string go by instinct. I didn't wait to see what happened, I just whipped another arrow out of my quiver and shot the next closest one. This one was a woman, her face twisted with rage. Dark circles were around her eyes, and her hands were twisted. Her fingers were black with strips of flesh hanging down from her nails.

I didn't need any more reason than her hands to shoot her in the face.

After my second shot I turned and ran, having put down our two closest pursuers. Trey had stopped a little further up the way than I had, and he was kneeling with his crossbow up. The string twanged, and a bolt split the chill air, whistling as it did so. The whistle ended with a meaty crunch as the bolt found a home in the skull of a third Tripper.

"Nice shot," I said, running by Trey.

"Thanks. Next time warn me before you do a little archery ballet," Trey said.

"Deal. By the way, we're out of road," I observed.

The street we had followed, called Justamere Road by the sign, ended abruptly into another street going east and west. The road was clear in both directions and promised easy passage for anyone taking that route. Unfortunately, that meant Trippers as well.

"Call it," Trey said, reloading his crossbow.

"It that a trail?" I said, pointing across the street.

Trey squinted. "Sure looks like it used to be one."

"Let's take it," I said. "We might get lucky and hit the river."

Trey brought his weapon up and fired again, this time killing a teenager who was wearing a very colorful shirt. "No such thing as luck with us, man; you know that."

"Let's move anyway," I said.

We took to the trail and were immediately swallowed up by trees and brush. There wasn't much in the way of cover since the winter had stripped the leaves off everything, but the trees were thick, and we were able to make good use of the trail that wound its way further and further north. The sun was full up now, and we made good use of the daylight. As we went, we kept an eye on our backs, and I was glad to see our pursuers were having a much harder time of the forest than we were. The ones who followed us directly were having the easiest time, but the ones on the fringe were not doing well in the tangling brush.

Through the trees we could see some houses and subdivisions, and given what was following us, Trey and I decided not to push our luck and try and lose them that way. God knows we probably would have opened another nest of the sick things.

We passed by two small ponds, and if it were summer and we had a boat we could have crossed the water and waited on the other side. Trippers weren't afraid of water, but swimming was beyond them. They usually walked in until they were over their heads and then they drowned. Dad told me the rivers were full of corpses during the bad times.

At the end of the second mile, or at least what I thought was the second mile, we stumbled out of the forest and smack into a river. It was about fifty to sixty feet across and looked like it was deep. The banks of the river were lined with trees, and there looked like the remains of another road following the river to the east.

"Sure would love to have a boat right about now," Trey said, looking back on our trail.

"I'm tired, too, but we need to keep moving," I said. "Maybe we'll find something along the way. People who lived this close to water like this had to use it from time to time."

"That makes sense," Trey said, falling in behind me.

The trail stayed close to the river, crossing a road at one point before dipping back into the trees. The river flowed silently beside us, a place of death and life, depending on how you treated it. We followed the trail, crossing from one side to the next, but always staying with the river.

Behind us, the Trippers stayed on our trail, never stopping, never resting. They were going to run us down soon, since we never could shake them, being as close as they were.

CHAPTER 47

We kept going and passed an uncountable number of houses. I was beginning to see where all the Trippers we had ever seen had come from. But the homes here were tiny and clustered close together. Living here must have been hard with no privacy to speak of.

"What's that?" Trey asked suddenly, pointing to a small structure. Leaning up against the side of the building was a silver, shell-like object.

"Our salvation," I said. "Come on!" I ran over to the object and flipped it over. My heart leaped with relief when I saw it was a small boat. Two oars fell out as I had tipped it, and they clattered noisily to the ground.

"Is this what I think it is?" Trey asked, picking up the oars.

"Yes, it's a boat," I said impatiently. "I know you know what a boat is."

"I'm just hoping it's not exhaustion playing with our heads," Trey said.

I took a serious look at my friend and realized he was played out. We had been moving for miles, and both of us were carrying heavy. Not to mention the fact that we were running for our lives, and the stress of that was taking its toll as well.

"Come on, let's get it to the water." I took one end and dragged the boat through the snow like a sled. It moved quickly until it suddenly stopped, jerking out of my hand and causing me to flip backwards. The bow I had on my pack jabbed me in the neck and in the back.

"Ouch. What the hell?" I said, painfully getting to my feet.

Trey traced a piece of rope from the boat to a small object that had lodged in a corner of the sidewalk that went around the building.

"Guess the anchor works," he said, holding the small weight up for me to see.

I just shook my head and let him toss the anchor inside with a dull boom.

We dragged the boat to the water and had a moment when we weren't sure what to do next. The river was lower than I expected it to be, and there was a pretty steep riverbank to get to it.

"Now what?" Trey asked. He looked down the path and saw the Trippers were getting closer by the second. "We have about two minutes, and then we're either running or dead."

I looked down the river and saw there was a spot where the riverbank sloped easily into the water. "Put the oars in and take my bow!" I said, shrugging off my pack and putting it in the boat. "Get in!"

Trey did what he was told, and I pushed him and the gear through the snow like a sled. The Trippers were about fifty yards behind me, and I could hear their wheezing in the cold air.

The boat was heavier than I thought, and I had to struggle through some thicker snow, but we got down the road towards the gentler slope, and I pushed Trey down the side. As the boat moved on its own, I gave another heave and then jumped in, adding to the momentum.

The boat slid down the riverbank and then fell a foot to the water, startling the two of us and causing me to nearly fall over the side. I caught myself just in time as Trey bopped me with an oar.

"Better get to paddling on your side," he said.

I took the long oar and pushed us away from the bank, easing us further into the current. As I pulled the oar back in, I watched the Trippers reach the river where we had slid in. Two of them fell into the water and sank like stones. The others milled a bit before a few more tried to walk out to get us. Apparently they forgot their Jesus shoes at home because they splashed into the cold water and sank out of sight.

We drifted away from them, and Trey figured out where the oars were supposed to go. Once we got the hang of things, we moved along pretty well. Trey rowed slowly, keeping us in the center of the river, and we stayed pretty much with the current. The boat was thankfully without holes, so we were safe and dry. Not much we could do about the cold, but we were dressed pretty well for that.

We watched the banks of the river slowly drift by, and the trees gave way to buildings and homes. Creaky looking bridges crossed overhead, and dark, humorless buildings stared down at us like the trespassers we were. On one bridge, there were about twenty Trippers looking at us as we floated away. Ten of them went into the water after us, never to rise again.

The sun sparkled on the water, and I noticed it was turning from bright white to a duller orange as it set. I nudged Trey and he jumped like he had been sleeping.

"Any thoughts on where we might want to sleep tonight?" I asked. "We sure aren't going to be home."

"I don't want to spend it on this boat, that's for sure," Trey said. "I need to be able to light a fire. I can't seem to get warm at all."

I looked closer at Trey, and he was actually in worse shape than I thought he was. If I didn't know better, I'd say he might be getting sick.

"All right. If we find a spot to get ashore we will," I said.

"When will we reach the wall?" Trey said.

"Not for miles," I said.

"Maybe we should head south now," Trey suggested. "We've lost the Trippers, and I haven't seen any more other than the ones on that bridge."

"All right. Let's find a spot to get out of the water," I said.

We rowed quietly through another area full of buildings, and on a sign over a road, I saw it was leading to I-57. Running my memory back a bit, I remembered seeing that same highway when my dad and I went east for that last time. If my head was clear, that road would take us within three miles of our own homes.

I said as much to Trey. "We need that road right there," I said, pointing.

"You got it," Trey said. He aimed us towards a section of the riverbank that had fallen over. The huge slab of concrete was hanging out over the water like a landing, and was just within reach of two young boys very far from home.

Trey swung the anchor and lodged it in a crack of the slab. The boat swung around, and Trey pulled us in. Looping the extra line around his arm, he climbed out of the boat, and then held the line while I took out our packs and weapons.

I climbed out, and Trey looked at me.

"What do we do with the boat?" he asked.

"If we lived closer to the water, I'd say let's take it with us," I said. "But since we don't, we may as well haul it up and leave it here."

Which we did. The hard part of pulling that boat out was keeping things quiet. There were a lot of homes and buildings around here that likely had Trippers inside, so we wanted to keep a more silent profile.

Once that was done, we headed up towards I-57 and started to make our way home, taking the highway.

CHAPTER 48

Dad told me that back when he as a kid they'd take what was called a "road-trip", which meant driving some crazy distance to go see something that wasn't available nearby. Sometimes it was to see another city; sometimes it was to see some kind of natural phenomenon. A lot of times people went to see their relatives that lived in other states. Dad said we had relatives that lived in Tennessee, but they were likely dead now.

No cars were on the highway, and it was easy walking. I'd have to remember to take Judy out to the highway once or twice. She'd get a kick out of being able to run as far as she wanted. We walked for what seemed to be a few hours, and the sun was definitely going down in a hurry. I figured we had about two hours of daylight left, so we'd better find some place to hole up for the night.

Trey was of the same mind, and we kept an eye out for likely places. The thing we hadn't counted on was how hard it would be to leave the highway. Most of the time we were well above the ground, and we'd have hurt ourselves pretty bad if we jumped. Several times we saw Trippers, and they tried to get over to us, but we were too high to get caught. We crossed a major highway that went east and west, and I tried to imagine all the places that road might hit if it wasn't for the wall. For the first time, I resented being penned off from the rest of the world, forced into a single state because of the damn Trippers. I wanted to see those far off places Dad talked about and look at the wild regions outside Illinois. I knew it was impossible, but I wanted to anyway.

"We can get off here and go into that tall building over there," Trey said as he pointed. "Doubt there's any activity in that place."

The building he had pointed out was a tall, stern-looking place. It was all of twenty stories tall, with blue glass windows and white concrete. At the top of the building was some sign that just had the letter B on it.

"Good a place as any," I said. I didn't like the look of it, but it was getting dark again, and I figured any place was better than an insane asylum.

We got off the road using a ramp and headed for the building. It was close to the highway, so it was just a matter of crossing the parking lot and getting to the place. Trey led the way, and we got inside by simply opening the door.

The lobby was huge, taking up at least three stories of the front of the building, High above us a glass structure caught the dying rays of the sun, sending little rainbows all over the interior. The floor was polished tile, which was a little dusty now, but must have been very nice when it was clean. Two tall trees were growing out of planters, and I was stunned to see they were in perfect health. It took a minute for me to realize they were fake.

Trey and I were enjoying the light show and the fact that the lobby was out of the cold that we didn't hear the Trippers that snuck up on us from the back of the lobby. I heard a soft wheezing sound, and when I started to turn around, I was hit full force by a charging Tripper.

"Trey!" I shouted, falling hard to the floor with a Tripper on my back. My bow went skittering away, out of reach. I tried to push off the floor, but the Tripper was lying on me, trying to punch me in the side and biting at my shoulder. My backpack strap was getting in its way, but that wasn't going to stop it for long.

"Trey!" I yelled. I twisted suddenly, slamming the Tripper to the floor. Its head cracked the hard tile floor and stunned it for a second. I shrugged out of my pack and scrambled away, crawling until I could get my feet under me.

The Tripper threw my pack away and lunged from the floor. He charged at me, and I dodged to the side, running in the opposite direction before facing him again. This time I pulled my knife from its sheath, and I held it like my father had taught me. With a live human, you hold it with the point down, edge toward the sky. With a Tripper, you held it in your fist, with the blade facing away from you and the edge to the outside. The uninfected died from cuts and stabs; the infected only died from a stab.

I didn't run; I just waited. I couldn't get away from this guy anyway, so it had to end here. A strange calm came over me, and I weighed in my mind what needed to be done. I glanced over at Trey, and he was sitting on the back of the Tripper that had attacked him, keeping him on the floor while the arms and legs of the Tripper kicked and swung. Trey pointed to his knife that was ten feet away and shrugged.

"Use a damn arrow, stupid!" I yelled.

The Tripper I was facing charged again, and as he passed, I swung hard with my knife, hoping to hit him in the heart. There was a meaty thud as my blade hit home, and suddenly the Tripper fell to the floor. My knife was wrenched out of my hand, and I looked at what had happened. Instead of hitting it in the heart, I had managed to hit it in the back of the neck. The blade had neatly severed its spine, paralyzing the creepy jerk. I went over to it, a little weak-kneed because the adrenaline rush was over, and yanked my knife out. The Tripper twitched its head, but could do nothing else. I went over to my pack and picked it up, shrugging it back on. I grabbed my bow, and with a little effort, sank a shaft into the back of the Tripper's head, ending it once and for all.

Trey got up a minute later, having dispatched his attacker as well. Neither of us had taken any bites which was a miracle, and my pack had minor tears where the Tripper had tried to chew on it, but it was still functional.

Trey looked at me, and I shrugged. "Sorry man, but you still had your quiver," I said, not really meaning it as an apology.

Trey smiled. "No worries. I forgot I had the thing with me. Once I got pushed over and found that thing trying to get me, I forgot all about my arrows."

"Let's find a place to sleep," I said. "It's nearly dark out."

Trey looked up. "Let's get to the top. I want to look out and see things from twenty stories up. Might never get the chance again."

That sounded good to me. I took my pack off and retrieved my Colt. I wasn't messing around with Trippers any more tonight. If there were any between here and the top floor, they were going to find I had a cure for their sickness in the form of a forty-five caliber pill.

CHAPTER 49

We climbed a stairwell that we found in the lobby that took us all the way to the top floor. The door opened up to a large space that was filled with desks and chairs and what had to be computers. We had a computer at the house that Dad just refused to get rid of. Maybe he hoped someday the power would get turned back on. The desks were separated by little walls so each person could have their own little office within the office. I personally thought it was kind of silly.

Trey walked over to the west side of the building and looked out the window. The sun was nearly down, and it was hard to see very much with the glare, but the world stretched out before us for miles and miles. We could see hundreds of homes of all shapes and sizes spread out along streets and side roads. Huge buildings grouped together told us where shopping centers used to be, and we could see the river fading off into the distance. I looked south and tried to see our houses, but the trees were too thick, and we couldn't have seen them anyway. I realized that there were many more Trippers out there than I ever realized, and for the rest of our lives, we were probably going to have to watch our backs and live with walls. Kind of depressing once I really thought about it.

When the sun finally set, Trey and I went over to the other side of the building and set up camp by the windows. Trey said he wanted to see the world when the sun came up. I couldn't argue with that.

I set up another candle again, and this time heated a little water in a small tin cup. Digging into my pack, I pulled out a little sack of dried corn. I crushed the corn under the pommel of my knife and tossed it into the water. Pulling out another sack, I added a handful of dried beans. A third sack yielded a handful of rice, and I stirred the mixture for a while, letting the water get to the ingredients. After a time, the mixture was soft enough to eat, the dried food having absorbed the water.

Trey put his own mixture together, and cooked his dinner off the same candle. Pulling out a metal box, Trey handed me a small hunk of bread and a piece of venison jerky. I opened a plastic tube and gave him a small apple, taking one for myself. We enjoyed a fairly good meal high above the ground.

After dinner Trey stretched out on a couch that we moved in from a small eating area. I found another couch in an office, and we dragged that one over as well.

Trey was asleep almost instantly, but I always took a little more time to fall asleep, especially in a place I wasn't familiar with.

I tossed and turned for a bit, then went over to the window. The sky was dark since a mess of clouds had come through as the sun had set. It was hard to see anything on the ground, but here and there I thought I saw movement.

Something caught my eye out to the east, and I stared for a long time. There was a small spot in the sky on the edge of the horizon that had a strange glow to it, like there was a huge fire blazing in the night.

Suddenly, there was a small pinpoint of light right at the bottom edge of the dark line of the horizon. It flashed for a second, disappeared, came back, and then was gone again. I stared for a long time, trying to see if that lone light would come back, but it never did. Instead, there were dozens of lights dancing on the horizon, blinking in and out, moving all over the place. Several lights went from north to south and then the opposite way. I had no idea what I was looking at.

My exhaustion finally got the better of my curiosity, and I stumbled back to my couch. Trey was snoring softly on his couch, oblivious to the world.

The last thought that hit me before I nodded off was a strange one.

'Open the gates. Lights. So many lights'

CHAPTER 50

We reached our homes at the end of the following day. Trey's father shook my hand in gratitude for helping his family, and I took a very excited Judy back to her stall at my house. She was happy to see me and even more happy to have her old place back all to herself. She got along with Pumpkin well enough, but she was like me. After a while, I needed my own space and my own company.

The house was the same as I had left it, but there was something different about it. I couldn't put my finger on what it was, but I was uneasy enough that I took to wearing my Colt wherever I went. I couldn't explain why, I just had this odd feeling like I was being watched. I covered my weapon with one of my dad's flannel shirts as I went about my daily routines, keeping as low a profile as possible.

I checked my trap lines and found that I had snared only a couple of rabbits. With the weather being as cold as it had been, the meat was still good. I checked the forest and found the tracks of several deer, as well as the tracks of two wolves. I guessed they might be looking for the guy who took out their leader.

A week after Trey and I had finished our mission, I returned to the house from the creek. I had to pull up a couple of buckets of water since snow wasn't easy to melt in decent quantities.

Right away I knew something was wrong. Judy was blowing and stamping, and she was not happy about something. I wasn't worried about a Tripper finding her. She could kill a Tripper without too much effort, but an uninfected person was another matter. I wondered if those men Trey and I had sent those Trippers after had escaped and somehow found their way back to us.

I went in through the garage and calmed Judy down. Looking around, I could see someone had been in here. Nothing was taken, but things weren't exactly in the place I had left them. It was like someone had come through, looked around, but found nothing of real interest.

I went into the house and looked around, keeping quiet and seeing if anything was missing. A Tripper would never had made it past Judy, so whoever was in here was normal— for the fact that they were in my house and didn't belong there.

The kitchen was clear, as was the dining room, and the front room. In the back room, I found my intruder.

She was looking at the bookshelves and was taking one down when I spoke.

"Most people wait by the gate and announce themselves," I said quietly.

Kim spun around and dropped the book, pulling a knife with her other hand. She dropped the knife to her side when she saw me.

"Josh! Oh my god! I didn't know you lived here," Kim said. "What a coincidence. How are you?"

"I'm fine, thanks. What are you doing here?" I asked. I didn't bother to contradict her story. I knew she knew I lived here. She'd been watching me for a while. Now that I thought about it, I figured she might had been staying in the house next door.

"Came through the area; thought this place looked safe," Kim said. She put the book back on the shelf and sheathed her knife. Her pack was in the corner, and by the look of things, she wasn't thinking about picking it back up any time soon.

"It is safe, and it's mine," I said. "Didn't you find any homes to live in where those big houses were?" I asked.

Kim shrugged. "Not the same. If I took over one of those houses, I'd have to build a wall, find supplies, find water, and make it work. I'd rather just find a place with all of that ready to go. Like this one." Kim looked at me. "I know you're all alone here, Josh, and I could use a place to settle into. We could be roommates," Kim said brightly, trying to sound enthusiastic.

"There's some houses down the road that could use some cleaning, and they already have a fence and supplies. Families are gone from them, so you'd not have any problem there," I said, hooking a thumb in my belt.

"Come on, Josh. You can't live here alone. You need company. We'd be a good team, "Kim said.

I shook my head. "Sorry Kim, but as much I would like to have you around, if for nothing but conversation, I'd rather just stay by myself."

Kim's voice turned hard. "Better be sure, *boy*. It's a dangerous world out there, and you're just a kid."

I didn't like where this was going. "I know how dangerous it is. My father told me every day how bad it is. He died saving me from it. It took my mother because it was so bad, and she couldn't handle it anymore. I just spent two days out there in the thick of it. All I've seen from you is to figure out how to run from it," I said, losing my temper a bit. I didn't like being called a boy, not when I was doing a man's job in keeping myself and my horse alive, too.

Kim nodded slowly, and when she spoke it was slow and deliberate. "I think I'll stay here whether you like it or not. I don't think I'm going to be leaving Josh, but I think you are." Kim's hand swept her knife out, and as she raised it her eyes got very wide and her face went very white.

The four clicks my Colt made as I eased the hammer back were very loud in the silence that followed.

"Drop it," I said quietly. Kim's knife clattered to the floor.

I moved over to the corner so I could keep Kim in front of me. "Get your gear and get out," I said.

Kim looked at me, and tears welled up in her eyes. "I'm sorry, Josh. I'm hungry, and I've been on my own for a year. I don't know how to act around people anymore."

I wasn't buying it. My dad had warned me that people revealed their true character with their actions, not their words, and if I hadn't had my gun, I fully believed Kim would have tried to kill me.

"Get moving. If you try anything, I'll drop the hammer," I said.

I knew I made the right choice when her tears dried up immediately, and she flashed me a look of pure hate.

Kim picked up her pack and stalked out, slamming the door on her way out. I followed to make sure she kept moving, and when she was on the other side of the wall she stopped.

I waited, not yet holstering my gun, but I was hoping she'd get a move on soon as it was cold today, and I wasn't wearing my coat.

She stood out there for a moment with her head up, then her chin dropped to her chest, and I could see her shoulders shake with real sobs this time. She turned around, and I could see the tracks of her tears on her face as sniffled at me.

"I don't know where to go," Kim said in a small voice.

I sighed as I holstered my gun. I was trusting my instincts on this one and hoped to hell I wasn't as dead wrong as I felt.

"Go into that house right there," I said. "It's on a good hill which will protect you on three sides. The fourth you're going to have to fortify. Trey and I will help you with that," I said.

Kim broke into a wide smile, and she ran over to my wall. "Thank you! Thank you!" she squeaked.

"Don't thank me yet. You have to drag the former residents out first," I said.

"Ew. Can you help with that?" Kim asked, looking at the house.

"Nope. That's the mortgage on the house. You want it, you pay it," I said, quoting one of my westerns.

Kim threw me a look, but she walked up to the house and went inside.

CHAPTER 51

It took three weeks, but between the three of us and some help from Trey's dad, we managed to clear out the house and build a serviceable wall around the vulnerable sides. The east side was completely open, but the way the land was configured no one, not even me, could easily climb up to the window, let alone get the leverage to break it. During that time, Trey and I got to know our new neighbor, and she got to know a few things about us. Trey and I taught Kim how to set trap lines, where the water was, and how to skin and gut the animals she caught.

It was funny when there was a pounding on the gate, and Kim as there with a dead rabbit, grinning like a loon and holding it up for me to see. I was proud of her for her success, and I think she felt like she could actually survive on her own without having to scavenge all the time. In the spring, Trey's mom promised to teach Kim how to can her own food and how to grow a good garden.

When the weather was warmer and the snow was in full retreat, Trey and I took the horses and headed back to that little sports store we had found in the winter. I still hadn't told Trey about the lights I had seen, and I still wondered if I had actually seen them at all. Maybe I had actually dreamed it. Part of me didn't believe it, but then I wondered if seeing those lights might have driven that other guy crazy.

I had asked Kim if she wanted to come with, but she was busy with her garden and yard, so she declined.

A warm breeze pushed us along the road, and I was carrying the compound bow we had found a month ago. I had discovered the bow's shorter limbs were perfect for shooting from horseback, and Judy loved the fact that I took her out more often. I was hunting larger game a lot more, and she was very helpful in pulling back full animals. It was also safer in that any Trippers we encountered, Judy was much better able to outrun them than I was.

We went past the asylum where Trey and I had spent that night, and it didn't look any better in the day. I was still curious about what they might have used the top floors for, but if I was honest with myself, I'd rather that remained a secret.

The landscape was different now that the snow was melting. Instead of being white, it was a lousy shade of brown. But even though it wasn't very pretty, it meant spring was coming and everyone, including the Trippers, felt it. We were seeing one every other mile; sometimes they were close, sometimes they were further away. I killed the ones that got too close, putting arrows in their hearts and dropping them. The compound bow made it easy, with the sights and all, and I had figured out how to adjust the strength of the pull so I had it at the edge of what I could manage.

"Still can't figure out why they die when I put an arrow in them, Trey," I said, putting the bow back behind me. I had a hook on a leather strap that the bow hung on. Judy didn't care, so I figured it was a good idea.

"No idea," Trey said. "I've seen several with bullet holes in them, but they're still walking around. Maybe they heal up if the holes are small, but if the thing causing the wound is stuck in there, they can't heal, and nature takes its course."

That was the best idea I'd heard. At least, it made the most sense.

"Is this the place?" I asked, pulling Judy up.

"Yep," Trey said. "The sign I threw in the bushes is still there."

We went through the store and picked up everything we had left behind. We filled bags with camping supplies, knives, arrows, and everything in between. I had two bags and Trey had two more, and I rigged the bags to act like saddlebags. Judy really put her ears back at me for the extra weight. I hoped we wouldn't have to run, but if we did, I was ditching our load.

We made it back to our homes before dark, and while Trey put Pumpkin away, I took the bags into the house to arrange the haul and see what we wanted to do with it.

While I was doing that, there was a hail from outside. I knew the voice and went out to let Kim into the yard.

"Hey, Josh! Do you have a hatchet I could borrow? I need to cut up some kindling, and the axe I have is not working as well as I want it to," Kim said.

"Sure, I think I can set you up better than that," I said. "Come on in."

Kim came in, and I was a little anxious to show her what I had. I think I needed someone to approve of what Trey and I had done. We went into the front room where I had laid out all of the stuff we had retrieved. Everything was categorized, and there were multiples of several items, including hatchets.

"Oh my god!" Kim said, clasping her hands to her mouth. "Where did you guys find all this stuff?" She picked up a lantern, put it down, picked up a knife, checked the edge, then put it down. She finally picked up a hatchet.

"Oh, this is perfect! Can I borrow it?" Kim asked, holding the hatchet close to herself.

"You can have it in trade," I said.

Kim cocked her head at me. "Trade for what?" she asked slowly.

"Information," I said.

"What kind of information?" Kim still looked at me with a funny look in her eye.

I had no idea what she might think I meant, but I wanted Trey to come over and hear it, too.

"Come back around an hour after sunset," I said. "Trey will be over, and we can have dinner. I'll tell you what I want to know then."

Kim gave me a half smile. "All right, Mr. Mysterious. See you later." As she passed me, she leaned over and gave me a quick kiss on the cheek. "Thanks."

I felt better than I had for a month. "You're welcome." I grinned like an idiot watching her walk back to her house.

CHAPTER 52

Trey came over after sunset, and we spent some time going over our haul and what we thought we could do with it. We decided not to try and have a store of any kind, mostly because we couldn't decide on who would run it. I thought we could trade the extra stuff for tools we didn't have, but Trey pointed out we could probably find whatever we needed for free.

"Sell it?" I asked.

"To who?" Trey replied. "And for what?"

I had to laugh. Here we were with a bunch of stuff that everyone could use, but no one really needed. "Maybe we'll just bring a little bit into town and see if there is anything to trade for," I said. "Maybe somebody has something we can't think of right now."

Trey laughed as well, and we worked ourselves up into a good fit of the giggles. Every time we stopped, one of us would snort or make a noise, and then we'd start all over again.

We were still giggling when Kim came over. She was carrying a small bundle which turned out to be a small loaf of bread. She was very proud of it, having made it herself. Trey's mother had shown her how to do it, and she was very eager to see what we thought of it.

Our dinner consisted of a stew made with rabbit meat, canned vegetables, and Kim's bread. The stew I had made a dozen times, and was pretty good if I did say so myself. I wish I could say the same thing about Kim's bread. Honestly, if I nailed that loaf to a stick, I could use it to brain half dozen Trippers without ever losing a crumb. Trey and I were too polite to say anything, though; we just held the bread in our mouths until it softened up a mite. Kim kept waiting for a response, and I tried to give her one, but the only thing I could get out was "Gouh."

"Does that mean 'Good', Josh?" Kim asked, taking a bite of her own creation. She worked in her mouth for a while and made several faces as she worked her jaws around it.

After about five minutes of chewing, we all got it down. I took the remainder of mine and dunked in the soup bowl, leaving it there for another five minutes before picking it up again to try a bite. When I did, there wasn't anything left in my bowl but meat and vegetables. The soaking helped, but not much.

"Well, it was my first try," Kim said.

"That's all right," Trey said. "You should have seen Josh's first attempt at skinning a rabbit."

"That bad?" Kim asked, smiling at me.

"Let's just say the rabbit would have looked better being eaten by a pack of wolves," I said, reddening a little under the collar.

We finished dinner and went to the large room off the kitchen. The stove had been fed recently, and the fire was warm. We pulled up chairs to be closer, and Trey brought out the little jar of cider he had 'borrowed' from his dad's supply. The cider was good when it was cold, but it was great when it was warm. Trey poured the jar into a coffee pot and put it on the stove to warm. When it was ready, we all had a cup, and in the warm glow of the fire and the fermented apple juice, I cashed in on the trade I had made with Kim.

"Kim," I said gravely, smiling.

"Josh," Kim replied, with equal, smiling gravity.

"That information I want from you."

"Okay. What's do you want to know?"

I looked at Trey before I looked back at Kim.

"What really happened when the Trippers came? I've only known what my dad told me, and it wasn't a lot. Things had already gone bad by the time I was born. But you were there. You know what happened. That's what I want to know," I said.

Kim looked at the two of us. She took a long drink before she settled back in her chair with her eyes closed tightly. After a few seconds, she leaned forward again and opened her eyes. She didn't look at us when she finally spoke; she was looking at a point in time twelve years ago.

"My parents were smart people, and we used to live in a big house right outside the city. I went to a nice school and had lots of friends. Our neighborhood looked a lot like yours, only there were kids all over the place, and no fences.

"I was a little girl when it all seemed to happen at once. I was even younger than you two. We'd been hearing reports about some kind of virus that came up through the streets; the junkies and the pot-heads were turning into rage monsters, tearing into people and ripping them up. Those that didn't die turned into the same infected people.

"My dad watched the news all the time, trying to get an idea of what was going on. My mother was more of the kind who thought the government would be able to take care of us; that we should just relax and trust, and we would be fine."

Kim paused for a minute, letting the memories come back. I could tell she'd pushed a few down deep that were just now seeing the light of day. After a long look into the fire, she started up again.

"The problem was we didn't know anything for sure! We were hearing reports, but there was nothing on the news, nothing! It was almost like we were being kept in the dark on purpose. We heard that the cities all over the country were full of Trippers, that people were dying by the thousands every day, and the only state that hadn't fully fallen was ours. So in order to keep some part of the United States alive, they sealed us off from the rest of the world, and we would have to fend for ourselves. Dad talked about duty and resolve and something else I didn't understand; all I know is he and my mother had a big argument over the rifle he had bought just the day before.

"Three weeks after the wall was built, the first Trippers started coming through our neighborhood. My girlfriend Jill was caught outside, and she was killed, torn to pieces by a small horde. Her parents tried to help her, but they were killed, too. People didn't really understand the disease or what it did to the people who caught it. They just didn't get it. No one really did," Kim said.

"I got a question," Trey said. "How did it spread so fast? We had always been told that you have to get bit to get the disease. Ain't no way all those Trippers could have suddenly sprung up from the streets just by being bit."

Kim smiled a little smile. "If you hadn't caught it in the first three months when everything was starting to go south in a hurry, then you weren't going to get it."

"Why not?" I asked.

Kim looked at me. "Because it was airborne."

CHAPTER 53

Everything came at me in a rush. My father, my mother. Oh my god, I killed my father. My mother died because my father was gone; I killed my father. I started to breathe heavily, and I had a hard time focusing. I couldn't hear what Kim was saying or Trey's responses.

A hand fell on my shoulder, and I looked up, right into Kim's eyes.

"You okay, Josh?" She asked.

"I killed my father," I said.

Trey looked at me for a second, and then he figured it out. "Oh, man. Josh, how could you have known?"

Kim rocked back into her chair. "Wait. What? What happened? What do you mean you killed your father?"

I couldn't formulate words. I waved hand at Trey. I could feel tears starting up, and my heart felt like it was going to fall out of my chest.

"Josh and his dad went out for a look at the wall, and on the way back, Josh's dad got bit by a Tripper. He thought he was turning and told Josh to end it for him. Josh did the right thing by his dad, and that was it," Trey said.

Kim shook her head. "You poor kid. How could you have known? Your dad was going to die, Josh, and it would have been extremely painful."

"What?" I said stupidly, my head still foggy.

"We finally figured out that Trippers are very sick themselves, and their bodies are literally walking virus farms. They have rotting meat and who knows what else in their mouths, along with the main virus which is a mutated form of ataxia," Kim said. "Your dad's system couldn't handle a load like that without heavy antibiotics, and he was *going* to die. People who get bit by Trippers will *always* die without antibiotics, and we ran out of those five years ago." Kim put a hand on my arm. "You saved your dad from a very prolonged, painful death. Never be sorry you did that. If I get bit, I hope someone will put me down."

I found I could breathe again, and it felt like my shoulders were a little lighter.

"Really? You're not just telling me this?" I asked.

Kim nodded. "My mother was bit by a lone Tripper in our back yard. My dad shot the Tripper, but it was too late. She lingered for three weeks literally screaming in pain until finally her heart gave out." Kim looked away again. "My father brought me to a neighbor's house and then he left. I never saw him again."

"What did people do when they realized they were on their own?" Trey asked.

Kim sighed. "People who lived in the city died. They couldn't get out; there were too many infected people there, and they had no way of getting food. Things got better the further you got away from towns, but then towns started building walls, and they started fighting for resources. My neighbors took me to a town north of here, and we lived there for three years before it got overrun by another town of bigger, meaner men. I was taken to live in the new town with the other children. My neighbors were massacred."

"Did you escape?" Trey asked.

"Day after I arrived," Kim said, with a little pride in her voice. "I took a knife, a pack of food, a bottle of water, and I took off. Been five years gone now."

"Where was that town?" I wanted to know.

"North of the river, just south of a big collection of highways," Kim said.

"Ever think of going back?" Trey asked.

"Not since the Trippers shredded it," Kim said.

We sat in silence for a while, just listening to the logs in the fire talk to each other. Every once in a while one would say something especially important, and punctuate its remarks with a shower of sparks and flame.

I voiced a question which had been on my mind for a while.

"What do you think is on the other side of the Wall?" I asked to no one in particular.

Trey spoke first. "Trippers."

Kim was gloomier. "Death. No one who has ever crossed over has ever come back."

I just nodded. "You're probably both right," I said.

We finished our evening, and since it was too late to send people home in the dark, I set up Trey and Kim in the extra bedrooms. The cider Trey had bought had really started to do a number on us, and we all were a little light-headed going into bed. I think I understood what Trey's dad meant when he called his cider the "Slow Riser".

In the morning, we went our separate ways, and I spent a good deal of time combing Judy and just thinking about things in general. One of the things I couldn't get out of my head was that crazy man's last words and what I had seen when we were up in that office building.

I went out to my lines, carrying my shorter bow. As I reached the top of the earthen dam, I looked east for a long time. My dad always told me that I needed a goal, something I had to try and achieve in life before I could move on to the next goal. It used to be surviving from day to day. But as I stood there feeling the sun on my back and hearing the whispers of the trees, I knew at that moment what my goal was.

I was going over the wall.

THE END

SEVEREDPRESS

⊙ facebook.com/severedpress

⊙ twitter.com/severedpress

CHECK OUT OTHER GREAT ZOMBIE NOVELS

Z BURBIA
by Jake Bible

Whispering Pines is a classic, quiet, private American subdivision on the edge of Asheville, NC, set in the pristine Blue Ridge Mountains. Which is good since the zombie apocalypse has come to Western North Carolina and really put suburban living to the test!

Surrounded by a sea of the undead, the residents of Whispering Pines have adapted their bucolic life of block parties to scavenging parties, common area groundskeeping to immediate area warfare, neighborhood beautification to neighborhood fortification.

But, even in the best of times, suburban living has its ups and downs what with nosy neighbors, a strict Home Owners' Association, and a property management company that believes the words "strict interpretation" are holy words when applied to the HOA covenants. Now with the zombie apocalypse upon them even those innocuous, daily irritations quickly become dramatic struggles for personal identity, family security, and straight up survival.

ZOMBIE RULES
by David Achord

Zach Gunderson's life sucked and then the zombie apocalypse began.

Rick, an aging Vietnam veteran, alcoholic, and prepper, convinces Zach that the apocalypse is on the horizon. The two of them take refuge at a remote farm. As the zombie plague rages, they face a terrifying fight for survival.

They soon learn however that the walking dead are not the only monsters.

SEVERED**PRESS**

 facebook.com/severedpress
 twitter.com/severedpress

CHECK OUT OTHER GREAT ZOMBIE NOVELS

900 MILES
by S. Johnathan Davis

John is a killer, but that wasn't his day job before the Apocalypse.

In a harrowing 900 mile race against time to get to his wife just as the dead begin to rise, John, a business man trapped in New York, soon learns that the zombies are the least of his worries, as he sees first-hand the horror of what man is capable of with no rules, no consequences and death at every turn.

Teaming up with an ex-army pilot named Kyle, they escape New York only to stumble across a man who says that he has the key to a rumored underground stronghold called Avalon..... Will they find safety? Will they make it to Johns wife before it's too late?

Get ready to follow John and Kyle in this fast paced thriller that mixes zombie horror with gladiator style arena action!

WHITE FLAG OF THE DEAD
by Joseph Talluto

Millions died when the Enillo Virus swept the earth. Millions more were lost when the victims of the plague refused to stay dead, instead rising to slaughter and feed on those left alive. For survivors like John Talon and his son Jake, they are faced with a choice: Do they submit to the dead, raising the white flag of surrender? Or do they find the will to fight, to try and hang on to the last shreds or humanity?

SEVERED**PRESS**

f facebook.com/severedpress
𝕏 twitter.com/severedpress

CHECK OUT OTHER GREAT ZOMBIE NOVELS

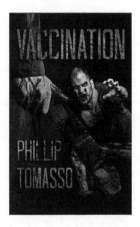

VACCINATION
by Phillip Tomasso

What if the H7N9 vaccination wasn't just a preventative measure against swine flu?

It seemed like the flu came out of nowhere and yet, in no time at all the government manufactured a vaccination. Were lab workers diligent, or could the virus itself have been man-made? Chase McKinney works as a dispatcher at 9-1-1. Taking emergency calls, it becomes immediately obvious that the entire city is infected with the walking dead. His first goal is to reach and save his two children.

Could the walls built by the U.S.A to keep out illegal aliens, and the fact the Mexican government could not afford to vaccinate their citizens against the flu, make the southern border the only plausible destination for safety?

ZOMBIE, INC
by Chris Dougherty

"WELCOME! To Zombie, Inc. The United Five State Republic's leading manufacturer of zombie defense systems! In business since 2027, Zombie, Inc. puts YOU first. YOUR safety is our MAIN GOAL! Our many home defense options - from Ze Fence® to Ze Popper® to Ze Shed® - fit every need and every budget. Use Scan Code "TELL ME MORE!" for your FREE, in-home*, no obligation consultation! *Schedule your appointment with the confidence that you will NEVER HAVE TO LEAVE YOUR HOME! It isn't safe out there and we know it better than most! Our sales staff is FULLY TRAINED to handle any and all adversarial encounters with the living and the undead". Twenty-five years after the deadly plague, the United Five State Republic's most successful company, Zombie, Inc., is in trouble. Will a simple case of dwindling supply and lessening demand be the end of them or will Zombie, Inc. find a way, however unpalatable, to survive?

 SEVERED**PRESS**

 facebook.com/severedpress
 twitter.com/severedpress

CHECK OUT OTHER GREAT ZOMBIE NOVELS

DEAD ASCENT
by Jason McPhearson

The dead have risen and they are hungry..

Grizzled war veteran turned game warden, Brayden James and a small group of survivors, fight their way through the rugged wilderness of southern Appalachia to an isolated cabin in the hope of finding sanctuary. Every terrifying step they make they are stalked by a growing mass of staggering corpses, and a raging forest fire, set by the government in hopes of containing the virus.

As all logical routes off the mountain are cut off from them, they seek the higher ground, but they soon realize there is little hope of escape when the dead walk and the world burns.

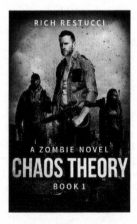

CHAOS THEORY
by Rich Restucci

The world has fallen to a relentless enemy beyond reason or mercy. With no remorse they rend the planet with tooth and nail.

One man stands against the scourge of death that consumes all.

Teamed with a genius survivalist and a teenage girl, he must flee the teeming dead, the evils of humans left unchecked, and those that would seek to use him. His best weapon to stave off the horrors of this new world? His wit.

SEVERED**PRESS**

 facebook.com/severedpress
 twitter.com/severedpress

CHECK OUT OTHER GREAT ZOMBIE NOVELS

RUN
by Rich Restucci

The dead have risen, and they are hungry.

Slow and plodding, they are Legion. The undead hunt the living. Stop and they will catch you. Hide and they will find you. If you have a heartbeat you do the only thing you can: You run.

Survivors escape to an island stronghold: A cop and his daughter, a computer nerd, a garbage man with a piece of rebar, and an escapee from a mental hospital with a life-saving secret. After reaching Alcatraz, the ever expanding group of survivors realize that the infected are not the only threat.

Caught between the viciousness of the undead, and the heartlessness of the living, what choice is there? Run.

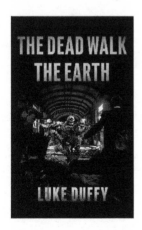

THE DEAD WALK THE EARTH
by Luke Duffy

As the flames of war threaten to engulf the globe, a new threat emerges.

A 'deadly flu', the like of which no one has ever seen or imagined, relentlessly spreads, gripping the world by the throat and slowly squeezing the life from humanity.

Eight soldiers, accustomed to operating below the radar, carrying out the dirty work of a modern democracy, become trapped within the carnage of a new and terrifying world.

Deniable and completely expendable. That is how their government considers them, and as the dead begin to walk, Stan and his men must fight to survive.

 SEVERED**PRESS**

f facebook.com/severedpress
◎ twitter.com/severedpress

CHECK OUT OTHER GREAT ZOMBIE NOVELS

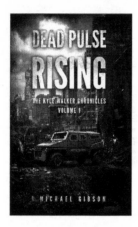

DEAD PULSE RISING
by K. Michael Gibson

Slavering hordes of the walking dead rule the streets of Baltimore, their decaying forms shambling across the ruined city, voracious and unstoppable. The remaining survivors hide desperately, for all hope seems lost... until an armored fortress on wheels plows through the ghouls, crushing bones and decayed flesh. The vehicle stops and two men emerge from its doors, armed to the teeth and ready to cancel the apocalypse.

TOWER OF THE DEAD
by J.V. Roberts

Markus is a hardworking man that just wants a better life for his family. But when a virus sweeps through the halls of his high-rise apartment complex, those plans are put on hold. Trapped on the sixteenth floor with no hope of rescue, Markus must fight his way down to safety with his wife and young daughter in tow.

Floor by bloody floor they must battle through hordes of the hungry dead on a terrifying mission to survive the TOWER OF THE DEAD.

51922067R00126

Made in the USA
Lexington, KY
09 May 2016